Stolen Souls

Stolen Souls

William Le Queux

MINT EDITIONS

Stolen Souls was first published in 1895.

This edition published by Mint Editions 2021.

ISBN 9781513280981 | E-ISBN 9781513286006

Published by Mint Editions®

 MINT
EDITIONS

minteditionbooks.com

Publishing Director: Jennifer Newens
Design & Production: Rachel Lopez Metzger
Project Manager: Micaela Clark
Typesetting: Westchester Publishing Services

Contents

I

The Soul of Princess Tchikhatzoff

Wrapped in furs until only my nose and eyes were visible, I was walking along the Nevski Prospekt in St. Petersburg one winter's evening, and almost involuntarily turned into the Dominique, that fashionable restaurant which, garish in its blaze of electricity, is situated in the most frequented part of the long, broad thoroughfare. It was the dining-hour, and the place, heated by high, grotesquely-ornamented stoves, was filled with officers, ladies, and cigarette smoke, while the savoury smell of national dishes mingled judiciously with those of foreign lands.

At the table next the one at which I seated myself were two persons, a man and a woman.

The former, who was about fifty, had a military bearing, a pair of keen black eyes, closely-cropped iron-grey hair, and a well-trimmed bushy beard. The woman was young, fair haired, and pretty. Her eyes were clear and blue, her face oval and flawless in its beauty, and she was attired in a style that showed her to be a patrician, wearing over her low-cut evening dress a velvet *shuba*, lined with Siberian fox; her soft velvet cap was edged with costly otter, and the *bashlyk* she had removed from her head was of Orenberg goat-wool. On her slim white fingers some fine diamonds flashed, and in the bodice of her dress was a splendid ornament of the same glittering gems, in the shape of a large double heart.

As our eyes met, there appeared something about her gaze that struck me as strange. Her delicately-moulded face was utterly devoid of animation; her eyes had a stony stare—that fixed, unwavering glance that one sees in the glazed eyes of the dead.

Having poured out a glass of the Brauneberger I had ordered, and taken a slight draught, I caught sight of a man I knew who was just leaving, and, jumping up, rushed after him. We remained chatting a few moments in the vestibule, and on returning, I sat down to my soup.

My neighbours were an incongruous pair. The man, who spoke the dialect of the South, was uttering words in a low, earnest tone with a curious, intense look in his eyes, and an expression on his dark, sinister features that filled me with surprise and repulsion. Notwithstanding his excited manner, his fair *vis-a-vis* remained perfectly calm, gazing at him wonderingly, and answering his questions wearily, in abrupt monosyllables.

Once she turned to me with what I thought was a glance of mute appeal. At last they finished their dessert, and when the man had paid the bill, he rose, exclaiming—

"Come, Agafia, we must be moving!"

"You—you must go alone," she said quickly, passing her hand wearily across her brow. "I have that strange sensation again, as if my brain is benumbed. My forehead seems on fire, and I can think of nothing except—except the enormity of my terrible crime."

And she shuddered.

"Fool! some one will overhear you," he whispered, with an imprecation. "You are only faint. The drive will revive you."

As she rose mechanically, he fastened her *shuba*, then, taking her roughly by the arm, led her out.

Finishing my meal leisurely, I afterwards sat for a long time over my tea and cigar, until I gradually became aware that my mind was wandering strangely, and a curious, apprehensive feeling was oppressing me, causing me considerable uneasiness. Tossing the cigar away, I pulled myself together, rose, and went out.

The thermometer was below zero, and in the keen night air my head felt better, yet as I walked along my senses seemed dulled. The one vivid impression, however, that remained on my mind was the calm, beautiful face of the girl who, by a slip of the tongue, had confessed to some mysterious crime. Walking on under the dark walls of the palace of Sergiei Alexandrovitch, embellished with its highly-coloured saints and heads of seraphim, I was suddenly amazed at seeing her standing before me. But a moment later I laughed heartily, when I saw that her form was a mere vagary of the imagination. The face, however, seemed so distorted by passion and indignation as to appear hideous, and in vain I endeavoured to account for its appearance.

On the Anitchkoff Bridge I paused, and as I leaned over to watch the skating carnival in progress, there was a movement behind me, and I heard words uttered in a low half-whisper—

"To-night. On the table!"

I turned quickly, but the unknown messenger was already some distance away, walking as quickly as his clumsy sheepskin would allow.

It was a summons from the Party of Political Right—the so-called

Nihilists! On one occasion, during my residence in the Russian capital, as correspondent of a London daily newspaper, I had been able to render the Terrorists an important service, and being in sympathy with their attempt to free their country from the terrible yoke of Tzardom, I sometimes attended their secret meetings.

The message I had received prompted me to take a drosky to an unfashionable little tea-shop a few doors from the entrance to the Gostinny Dvor Bazaar. Having seated myself, and ordered a cup of tea and a cigarette, I leaned my arms on the little round marble table, and, without attracting notice, proceeded to examine it minutely.

Strange as it may seem, this table was the private notice-board of the Nihilists. The proprietor was a member of the Circle, and this was considered one of the safest means of communication. In a few moments I discovered what I sought; a line in English, very faintly traced with a lead pencil, which read, "Come at eleven to-night, certain." For nearly an hour I remained smoking and chatting with the genial proprietor, then, after rubbing out the message, bade him adieu and left.

Shortly before eleven I strolled down one of the narrow, squalid streets that led to the Neva, halted before a little bakery, and having rapped three times at a side door, was admitted. Passing to the end of a long, dark passage, I bent, groped about until I found an iron ring in the floor, and pulled up a large flap, from beneath which came a flood of light. Then I descended the ladder, and, walking into an underground kitchen, found myself in the presence of the Revolutionary Executive Committee.

As I glanced round quickly, I saw a stranger—a woman, with her back turned towards me, and holding in her hand a bright, keen knife. She stood looking up at the *ikon* upon the wall. The president from his seat at the head of the table had apparently been addressing her.

"I agree to the conditions," she was replying, in Russian, in harsh, strained tones. "I bind myself irrevocably, by my solemn oath before this holy picture, to strike any such blow for liberty as the Circle may direct."

There was something in her form that struck me as curious, and as she slowly raised the knife to her lips, and kissed the thin, double-edged blade, I rushed across and looked into her face.

It was the woman I had noticed in the Dominique! She had taken an oath to commit murder at the bidding of the Revolutionists! There was the same fixed look in her eyes, the same blank, expressionless countenance, and as she turned and faced the council of desperate conspirators, her teeth were firmly set and her bejewelled hands tightly-clenched.

As her eyes met mine, I fancied she started, but the words of the president attracted her attention.

"It is enough," he said solemnly. "To-morrow you will receive instructions. You have joined us, therefore never forget that the punishment inflicted on those who divulge our secret is always swift and decisive—death!"

A shudder ran through her, the knife fell from her grasp, and she reeled and would have fallen, had not an elderly, grey-haired woman jumped up from her seat and caught her.

In a few moments, however, she recovered, and the pair walked slowly out.

When they had left, I inquired the name of the mysterious stranger, but all information was refused. Secrecy is one of the chief tenets of the Nihilistic creed, and frequently members of the same Circle do not know one another. The Terrorist organisations are most elaborate and far-reaching, and the more I have known of their operations, the more wonderful they have always seemed. The business of the Executive with me was unimportant—merely to give me some information which I might send to London, and which, when published in my journal, would be calculated to take the police off the scent of a fugitive conspirator who was being diligently sought for by the ubiquitous members of the Third Section of the Ministry of the Interior.

When I left, half an hour later, I went straight to my bachelor lodgings in a tall and rather gloomy house on the other side of the Moika. Lighting a cigarette, and drawing my armchair close to the stove, I sat for a long time in my dimly-lighted sitting-room, pondering over the events of the evening. How long I sat there I have no idea, but I was aroused by distinctly hearing a woman's shrill scream. At the same time, I felt a tight pressure on my right wrist, as if it were being held by bony fingers, and on my throat I felt a strange, cold sensation, as if a knife had been drawn across it.

Again I was mystified on discovering that I was alone; that it was nothing but a weird sensation! Yet, on removing the green shade from my reading-lamp, and going over to the mirror, I saw upon my throat *a thin red line*, while upon my wrist were three red marks that had apparently been left by unseen fingers!

During the weeks that followed, I seemed filled with a terrible dread of some utterly vague danger, and before my eyes came frequent visions of the pale, handsome face of the beautiful woman who had allied herself with the most dangerous group of the Narodnaya Volya. Was there, I wondered, some mysterious affinity between us? So puzzled was I to account for the strange phenomena, and the fact that the curious marks upon my wrist still remained, that I began to fear that the periodical fits of passion and despair were precursory of madness.

Lounging aimlessly along the streets in the hope of meeting her, I was walking one afternoon along the English Quay, when a drosky drove swiftly past, and pulled up before one of the great palaces that face the Neva. A woman, wrapped in costly furs, alighted, and in a moment I recognised her. As I approached, she halted, with her eyes fixed upon me, her mouth slightly open, and the same curiously blank expression on her countenance. At first I was prompted to stop and speak, but the tall man-servant in livery who had thrown open the great door looked down upon me with suspicion, therefore I hesitated, and walked on.

As I brushed past her, I thought I heard a long sigh, and, turning, I was just in time to see her enter the palace, saluted by the gigantic *dvornik*.

Stumbling blindly on for a few hundred paces, I met a man I knew, and, pointing out the house, asked him who lived there.

"The woman has enmeshed you, eh?" he suggested, laughing. "Well, you are not the first who has been smitten by her extraordinary charms."

"What do you mean?" I asked.

"Flirtation is a dangerous pastime here, in Petersburg," he replied, shrugging his shoulders ominously. "Especially so if one's idol is Agafia Ivanovna, the Princess Tchikhatzoff."

"Princess?" I echoed, in surprise.

Then, linking my arm in his, I begged him to tell me what he knew of her. But he only replied—

"I really cannot tell you anything, *mon cher*, except her name. Ugly rumours were once afloat, but perhaps the least said of her the better."

And, waving his hand and wishing me a hurried adieu, he went on.

A month later, having received instructions from London to proceed to the cholera-infected districts of Vologda, in order to describe the hospitals, I had obtained the necessary permit from the Ministry of the Interior, and one evening had taken my seat in the mail train for

Moscow. Scarcely had I arranged my traps and prepared for the long night journey, when a rather shabbily-attired female appeared at the carriage door.

"M'sieur," she exclaimed in a soft, musical voice. "It is M'sieur Wentworth that I address, is it not?"

Replying in the affirmative I alighted.

"You are going to Pavlova, in Vologda?" she said in broken English. "I—I am in a great difficulty—a great danger threatens me. If you would only render me a service, I should indeed owe my life to you."

"What can I do?" I asked.

"I have here a message to a—a friend who is lying ill of cholera in the hospital at Pavlova;" and she drew forth a letter from under her faded shawl.

"You wish me to deliver it?"

"Yes," she replied anxiously. "Were I able to travel, I would not ask this favour; but only the journalists are allowed to pass the cordon, and the post is suspended for fear of infection."

I took the letter slowly from her hand, and as I did so, was amazed to discover that on her slim white wrist there were three red marks, exactly similar to those I bore!

"I shall be pleased to act as your messenger," I said, placing the letter in my pocket; "you may rest assured it will be delivered safely, Princess."

"You recognise me, then?" she cried, starting back. "I—"

But her sentence remained unfinished, for the train was moving off slowly, and I had barely time to scramble in without bidding her adieu.

The mid-winter journey by sleigh through the remote, plague-stricken district, where poverty, disease, and death were rife on every hand, was a terrible experience. The distress and suffering I witnessed is photographed indelibly on the tablets of my memory. Not without difficulty, I one night found Nikanor Baranovitch, the addressee of the letter, who was lying on the point of death in the filthy log-built hospital. He was young, dark-haired, emaciated, but still conscious. When I handed him the missive, he tore it open eagerly and read it by the aid of the guttering candle I held.

Suddenly his face was convulsed by anger, and, crying, "Agafia— Agafia!" he uttered fearful imprecations in Russian. Then, crushing the letter in his hand, he thrust it into the flame of the candle, and in a moment the flimsy paper was consumed.

Gasping a word of thanks to me, and crying for the vengeance of heaven to descend upon some person he did not name, he sank wearily back upon the dirty straw pallet, and a few moments later had passed to the land that lies beyond human ken.

Two years had gone by. I was back again in England, writing descriptions of events at home, and holding myself in readiness to journey to any quarter of the globe, should occasion arise.

Frequently in my day-dreams the countenance of the Princess Agafia Ivanovna passed before me, always serious, always haggard, always intense.

When, after my journey through Vologda, I returned to the capital, the Tchikhatzoff Palace was closed, and the only information the burly *dvornik* would vouchsafe was that the Princess had gone abroad.

I longed to penetrate the mystery surrounding her, and obtain some explanation of the extraordinary coincidence of the marks upon her wrist and mine. I had never been entirely myself since first seeing her. Some strange, occult spell seemed to enthrall me, for the phenomena I had experienced were remarkable, while the varied mental sensations were utterly mystifying.

Horribly morbid thoughts constantly oppressed me. Sometimes they were of murder, which I felt impelled to commit, even though the very suggestion was repugnant. At others, in moments of blank despair, I contemplated the easiest modes of suicide; while through all, I cherished a deadly hatred towards some person of whose identity I had not the remotest notion.

In the months that had elapsed after returning to England, I had gradually grown callous to mental anguish; yet the bodily pain I frequently experienced in the wrists and across the forehead was remarkably strange, inasmuch as livid marks would sometimes appear on my arms without any apparent cause, and disappear as suddenly as they came.

Through the hot August days I was idling in that part of Norfolk that is justly termed Poppyland, making my headquarters at a farmhouse near Cromer. I had been unusually perturbed regarding Agafia Ivanovna, and such an intense longing to see her had seized me, that I even contemplated returning to Petersburg.

One very hot afternoon, while sitting on the bench outside the house calmly smoking, some unknown force prompted me to rise and set out for a long walk along the cliffs. I had no motive for doing this, yet a lichen-covered stile, nearly five miles in the direction of Yarmouth, was fixed in my mind as my destination, and I felt myself compelled to reach it.

The sun blazed down mercilessly, notwithstanding the cool breeze that had sprung up, and sparkling waves were breaking with sad music on the shingly beach. Engrossed in my own thoughts, I had sped on, and was just approaching the stile, when the rustle of a woman's dress startled me, and I saw a graceful form clad in cream-coloured serge, with a bright ribbon at the waist, standing before me.

I recognised her features. It was Agafia!

"You, Princess?" I cried in astonishment, grasping her hand.

But she uttered a low scream, and, twisting her fingers from mine, dashed swiftly away. I was unable to overtake her, for, taking a desperate leap, she alighted on a projecting rock, and, scrambling down among the bushes, descended the precipitous face of the cliff and disappeared.

Not daring to follow, I remained breathless and bewildered for about half an hour, and at length turned my heavy steps again towards Cromer.

WHILE WALKING IN LONDON'S *AL FRESCO* pleasure exchange, the Row, one bright spring afternoon, exchanging salutes with those I knew, a brilliantly-varnished carriage, drawn by a magnificent pair of bays, suddenly passed me. Notwithstanding the rapid pace at which it was driven, I caught a glimpse of the tip of a tiny bronze shoe stretched against the cushion of the front seat, the fold of a light fawn dress, and under a lace-fringed sunshade a fair face—the face of Agafia Ivanovna, Princess Tchikhatzoff.

Until the equipage turned out of the Park, I kept it in sight; then I jumped into a hansom, and followed, until I watched her alight and enter one of the largest houses in Queen's Gate. On inquiry, I ascertained that the house had been taken furnished for the season by a young foreign lady, whose name nobody seemed to know.

That evening, after dining at the club, I sat in the smoking-room, shrinking with horror from some terrible deed that I seemed forced to commit. Then gradually there crept over me that strange attraction that drew me irresistibly towards her; until at last, unable to remain, I put on my hat and drove to the house.

"I wish to see the Princess," I said, giving my card to the grave, elderly man-servant who opened the door.

Bowing, he ushered me into a small, well-furnished room and disappeared. The moment he had gone, I heard voices speaking rapidly in Russian in the next apartment. Agafia was addressing some man, and I thought I heard her utter my name, and refuse to see me. The rooms communicated by means of folding-doors, and, determined to speak with her, I turned the handle and entered.

The scene that met my gaze was only momentary, but it was one of tragedy. In a low lounge chair a young man was sitting, calmly smoking a cigarette. He had blonde hair, but his face was turned from me. Stealthily Agafia crept up behind him, her face distorted by the same terrible look of vengeance that I had sometimes seen in my weird day-dreams. In her uplifted hand something gleamed in the lace-shaded lamplight. It was the knife upon which she had taken the *ikon* oath in Petersburg.

"Princess! At last!" I cried, rushing forward in an endeavour to prevent her from striking the deadly blow at her unsuspecting visitor.

At that moment, however, I felt my hands gripped tightly, and a man flung himself before me. With an imprecation, I tried to push him aside, for I had instantly recognised him as the man who had dined with the Princess at the Dominique.

My senses seemed paralysed. With one hand he held me, and with the thumb and finger of the other he pressed my temples so tightly that I became dazed. For a moment I was conscious of his sinister face peering into mine, and of a peal of harsh, demoniacal laughter that rang through the room. Then I knew no more.

When I recovered consciousness, I found myself lying in bed in a long hospital ward, with the kind face of my friend, Dr. Ferguson, a specialist in mental diseases, looking down upon me.

I had, he told me, been found by the police early one morning lying in a back street in Kensington in a state of collapse, owing to injuries I had received on the head. For a week I had been delirious, and no hope had been entertained for my recovery; but at last I had rallied, and was now gaining strength.

He questioned me, apparently in order to ascertain if my brain had been affected; but it was remarkable that my mind was much clearer than hitherto.

It was many days before I was able to rise, but at last, when I was allowed to go out, I related to him all the circumstances surrounding the mysterious Princess.

Being much interested, he consented to accompany me to the house, and late that evening I placed my revolver in my pocket, and together we took a cab to the corner of Queen's Gate.

Dismissing the man, we walked together to the house, only to find the shutters up and the place deserted. Our knocks and rings having been unanswered, we descended to the area, and after considerable difficulty entered by the kitchen window. By the aid of a candle we had brought with us, we searched the house, which we found still furnished, although unoccupied, and on the carpet of the room in which I had seen Agafia was a great dark stain—the stain of blood. Was it mine, or that of the unknown victim?

Ascending to the floor above, we opened the door of the drawing-room, and on glancing round the great, handsome apartment, our eyes fell upon an object that caused us both to start back in amazement.

Attired in a long, loose gown, and chained by her wrists to one of the polished granite columns, was Agafia!

With her hair unbound, she had sunk at the base of the pillar, and was apparently dead. Evidently she was a prisoner, for the empty jug and plate standing near told their own tale.

As in a moment of passion I bent to kiss her, Ferguson, who had placed his hand upon her breast, took out a lancet and made a slight incision in her arm.

"There is yet life," he said.

"Thank heaven!" I cried. "We must save her."

Opening her eyes, he took the candle and looked intently into them. They still had a fixed, stony stare, and there seemed a film upon them.

Then the doctor, with his forefinger and thumb, stroked her forehead in a downward direction, pressing her temples, saying—

"You shall now awake and feel exactly as you were before that villain placed you under his influence. Come, rouse yourself! Rouse yourself!"

Several times he repeated this, until at length her eyes twitched, her face flushed, and she gradually became perfectly conscious, answering the doctor's questions quite rationally. But at me she glanced shyly, and blushed.

"She remembers nothing distinctly since she was hypnotised," Ferguson said, "therefore you are a stranger."

I endeavoured to explain that I had delivered the letter she entrusted to me; but she shook her head, saying—

"I only saw you once, in the Dominique Restaurant in Petersburg, when you drank the wine over which Petrovitch Delianoff had made passes during the few moments you were absent."

Ferguson, who was one of the greatest English authorities on hypnotism and a student of the occult, eagerly asked what the man had done.

"He touched my forehead quickly in a curious way," she answered, "and he afterwards dipped his finger in the wine, saying, 'Your sensibility and soul will now leave you and be transferred to this glass of wine. In future you will feel nothing.' Since that time I—I seem to have been in a long dream; I can remember nothing distinctly."

"Ah! I now understand," exclaimed my friend, raising the candle and looking into my eyes. "The man has experimented successfully upon you with the novel method of producing hypnosis recently discovered by Charcot at La Salpetriere. Remarkable as it may seem, it is, nevertheless, possible to transfer by suggestion the sensibility of hystero-epileptic subjects to any liquid. On drinking the wine, you absorbed her sensibility, and her very soul thus transferred to you, produced the mysterious affinity of thought and deed. The very singular coincidence of the marks upon your wrists, and the curious magnetic force that impelled you towards her, are nothing more than demonstrations of the powerful psychical influence of the mind on the body."

"What can have been the motive for all this?" I exclaimed, when, after considerable difficulty, we had broken the chains and led her to a chair.

"The motive was gold," she answered in a weak voice. "I—I am the victim of the man Delianoff. Mine has been a tragic career. Three years ago I loved Nikanor Baranovitch; but, although only eighteen, my mother compelled me to marry the Prince, who was nearly forty years older than myself. It is true he idolised me, but I cannot say that I experienced the least regret when, five months later, he died, leaving me all his wealth. Then, alas! my unhappiness commenced. The management of the estate was left to Delianoff, and there was a clause in the will which provided that if I died, or married Nikanor, the property should go to Vladimir Lemontzeff, a nephew of the Prince's who was an *attache* at the Embassy in London.

"Almost as soon as the Prince was buried, Delianoff proceeded to place me under his influence, for, my mother and most of my near relations being dead, I was utterly alone. The scoundrel was an accomplished hypnotist, and in order to further his villainous scheme, he put cruel rumours in circulation which caused Petersburg society to shun me. His irresistible power of fascination I was unable to withstand, and by hypnotic suggestion he has caused me to hand over to him the greater part of my fortune. He kept me constantly in his thrall by threatening to give information to the police that I had committed murder. This crime he had suggested to me, causing me to believe that I had actually stained my hands with blood. Just at that period I saw you in the Dominique, and, as I have already explained, he practised on you one of his devilish experiments. He was a Nihilist, and on that night he used his influence to induce me to attend a meeting alone, and swear to kill whoever the Executive decided should be removed. Soon afterwards I heard of Nikanor's illness in Pavlova, and you were good enough to convey to him a letter in which I told him how Delianoff had attempted to cut my throat, and how utterly helpless I was in his hands."

"Nikanor died, and could not save you," I observed sorrowfully.

"Yes," she sighed; "Delianoff's motive for getting me to take the oath was as ingenious as his other villainies, for, when his plans were complete, he brought me to London, invited Vladimir here, and then, by the exercise of his occult power, he made me believe that the Prince's nephew was the man the Executive had ordered me to kill. But you saved me, for just as I was about to strike the fatal blow, you entered. Delianoff at that moment came behind you, and, with his curious touch, insinuated in your brain the image of sleep. Of what afterwards occurred I know nothing, for I fainted.

"This scoundrel, who had planned that I should kill Vladimir and afterwards commit suicide, in order that his villainy should not be exposed, was mad with rage at the failure of his plot. When I regained consciousness, he dragged me about the room, brandishing a knife and threatening to murder me; but at last his anger cooled, and his demoniacal ingenuity devised a terrible torture. My passive will was still under his influence, and I could not escape or utter cry when he locked the fetters upon my wrists and chained me to yonder column. For several days he came regularly with food and water, but four days ago, after telling me how he had obtained possession of all that belonged to me, he laughed derisively, and said he should leave me to die of starvation."

"Yes; we were only just in time," the doctor remarked, feeling her pulse, with his eyes upon his watch. "You would have been dead to-morrow."

The Princess had no friends in London, therefore I gave up my chambers to her, taking up quarters at a neighbouring hotel, while the hospital nurse I engaged attended her until she fully recovered.

She can never recover the bulk of her fortune; nevertheless she has the satisfaction of knowing that Delianoff speedily met with his deserts.

Although ostensibly a Nihilist, it was ascertained that he acted as a spy in the pay of the Secret Police. His end was befitting a coward and a traitor, for while assisting in an attempt to wreck the Winter Palace, he handled a bomb carelessly, with the result that it exploded and killed him.

Some are of opinion that, being an informer, the vengeance of the Narodnaya Volya fell upon him, and I incline to that belief.

II

The Golden Hand

Ramblings, erratic and obsession-dogged, had taken me to Bagneres de Luchon, over the snow-capped Pyrenees by the Porte de Venasque to Huesca, thence to quaint old Zaragoza and Valencia, and in returning from Madrid I found myself idling away a few days at San Sebastian, that gay and charming watering-place which somebody has termed "the Brighton of Spain." The month was July, the town was filled with Madrileftos attracted by the excellent bathing, and glad to escape the stifling heat and dust of the Castellana or the Calle de Alcala, while the shell-like Concha, or bay, was given up to the *campamento* of bathing-tents.

From my seat in the porch of the Fonda de Ezcurra I gazed upon the beautiful Bay of Zurriola, with its twinkling lights, crowded with a thousand fantastic shadows; I heard the creak of the row-locks and the plashing of oars, and the laughter of girls; and in the deep gloom not far away the faint music of violins and mandolines trembled in the air. So still was the night that the regular throbbing of paddle-wheels from a steamboat not yet visible formed a rumbling undertone to all the other sounds, and the summer moon bathed all things in its mystic light, throwing far out over the water into the Bay of Biscay a bright, shining pathway.

Across this path boats glided from time to time; on the asphalte walk at the edge of the beach fair flirtatious little dames in graceful mantillas passed to and fro, and as I lit a cigarette, I dreamed and dwelt upon the future.

Presently a neat-ankled waiting-maid came out and handed me a telegram which she said had arrived during dinner, and I rose, sauntered over to where the great light was placed above the door, and opened the dispatch. It gave me satisfaction, for it was an order from the journal I represented to remain there, and transmit by telegraph daily what fresh intelligence I could gather with regard to the political crisis through which Spain was at that moment passing. By reason of the Queen-Regent, the young King, and the Court having left Madrid for San Sebastian a week earlier, the *locale* of the crisis had been removed from the capital, and among those staying at my hotel were Senor Canovas del Castillo, the Conservative leader, Senor Novarro Reverter, Minister of Finance, and Senor Villaverdi, ex-Minister of the Interior, besides several members of the Cortes. In these circumstances the prospect of a week or two at one of the most charming of European health-resorts was by no means distasteful, especially as I saw that I should experience but little difficulty in obtaining such information regarding the situation as I required. A rigorous censorship had been established by the Government over all telegraphic messages sent out of the country, therefore it would be necessary for me to cross the frontier into France each day, and send off my dispatch from Bayonne.

Thrusting the telegram into my pocket, I lit a fresh cigarette, and lounged away down the Avenida de la Libertad to the Calle del Pozzo; the fine tree-lined promenade behind the Casino, where the life and gaiety of the town had assembled. Under the bright electric rays crowds of well-dressed promenaders were strolling slowly up and down, listening to the strains of a military band, and ever and anon, when the music paused, the chatter and laughter mingled in a din of merriment with the jingle of the many gaily-lit cafes in the vicinity. Carried to and fro the length of the asphalte by the ebb and flow of promenaders, I spent a pleasant hour watching the life around me, and enjoying the cool air after the heat and burden of the glaring day. San Sebastian is noted for the beauty of its female population, and, indeed, I am fain to admit that I saw more beautiful women during that brief hour than it had ever been my lot to meet at Vichy, Etretat, Royat, Arcachon, Biarritz, Nice, or any of the other favoured spots where Dame Society allows her world-weary children to disport themselves at certain seasons. Spanish women know how to dress, but the women of San Sebastian rely not upon the manipulation of the fan nor the arrangement of the mantilla to attract; they are naturally graceful in gait and fair of face.

Two figures in that crowd riveted my attention, but, alas! only for a moment. I gazed upon them, but next instant they were gone, swallowed in that ever-shifting vortex of laughter-loving pleasure-seekers. Both were attired in black, one an elderly lady with white hair, upon whose refined face care had left deep furrows; the other a tall, graceful girl, scarcely more than nineteen, evidently from the South, whose calm, serious face was even more strikingly handsome than those of the many beauties about her. The *chevelure* had evidently been arranged by a maid of the first order; the mantilla she wore, graceful in every fold, gave to her clear olive complexion an essentially soft and feminine look; her dark eyes were large and languishing, and there was that peculiar grey tint upon the skin that when natural in women of the South is so unusual and so artistic.

For a second, unnoticed by her, I gazed in admiration, but she passed on and was lost. Turning a few moments afterwards, I sped back in the hope of overtaking her and again feasting my eyes upon her incomparable beauty, but though I searched the crowd for fully half an hour, I was compelled to relinquish my self-imposed task, turning at last into the Casino, where, over cigarettes and coffee, I sat chatting to a loquacious old captain of artillery upon the political crisis until the musical carillon of San Vicente chimed the midnight hour. Then, wishing my companion "*Buenas noches*," I rose and strolled back to my hotel, haunted by the sad, sweet face that had passed and vanished like a shadow.

But I had work before me. The relations between England and Spain were strained, and diplomatic negotiations regarding some incidents in Morocco and in Cuba had been rendered more difficult on account of the unexpected overthrow of the Ministry. The British Government was more interested in the affairs of Spain than it had been for many years, so the British public were eager for the latest intelligence; therefore, when I retired to my room, I was compelled to sit far into the night, writing by the light of a guttering candle all I knew, and recording every rumour anent the complex questions.

Those who have wandered over the yellow sands of San Sebastian well know how picturesque is the view across the Bay of Zurriola. It was upon this scene I gazed on opening my windows on the following morning. Beyond the broad Plaza, lined on three sides by handsome houses, the sunlit waters of the Bay of Biscay rolled in upon the shore, wave after wave of transparent emerald breaking in long lines of snowy foam. White villas gleamed from among the foliage on the hillsides, and high brown cliffs rose from right and left, against which the rollers, roaring and surging, dashed and went up in columns of spray.

Swallowing my coffee, I went out—not, however, before I had made a gratifying discovery; namely, that the room next mine, communicating by a locked door, was the private sitting-room of Senor Canovas del Castillo, the statesman upon whose political actions the eyes of Europe were at that moment centred. Success in journalism depends a good deal upon luck, and to accidental incidents I attribute any good fortune

I have enjoyed in obtaining exclusive and reliable information in various holes and corners of the Continent where I have had to compete with the resident correspondents of Reuter's, the Havas, and the Central News agencies. I had walked across the Plaza de la Constitucion, wondering how I could best turn this fortuitous circumstance to account, when suddenly I found myself before the grey facade of Santa Maria, and almost involuntarily I entered. The air was heavy with incense, and the church was in semi-darkness—a chiaroscuro that was exceedingly striking and effective. There was, however, little of interest beyond the heavily-gilded and somewhat tawdry altars, which are the feature in most Spanish churches, and I was just about to leave when the silence was broken by loud sobbing close to me. I had believed myself alone in the place, but on gazing round in surprise, I saw within a few yards of me, half hidden by one of the great stone columns, a female figure kneeling before one of the altars, with her face buried in her hands, sobbing as though her heart would break. I was turning away, leaving the lonely worshipper to her grief, when the dress, the softness of outline, and the flawless complexion seemed strangely familiar. Next instant I recognised her as the girl I had passed in the crowd, and whose beauty had so impressed me.

Upon the stones she was kneeling in abject despair. In her dark hair she had placed a crimson rose, and her delicate white hands, upon which some bright gems glistened, were wet with bitter tears.

My feet fell noiselessly upon the matting, and she was unaware of my presence, until, placing my hand lightly upon her shoulder, I bent, exclaiming in French:—

"Mademoiselle is unhappy! Is there no assistance I can render?"

She started, raising her pale, pensive face to mine in surprise. Then in sorrow she shook her head.

"M'sieur is very kind," she answered, in a voice that betrayed a poignant grief. "Words of sympathy may lighten one's burden of sorrow, but nothing can heal a broken heart."

"It mainly depends on how the fracture was caused," I answered, smiling, and, grasping her tiny hand, assisted her to rise.

She brushed the dust from her dress, dashed away her tears, and, turning to me, said—

"I have heard that gaiety is efficacious—sometimes."

"Until I know the cause, I cannot prescribe for the effect," I replied, as I held open the door and she passed out into the sunlight.

"Ah, m'sieur," she sighed bitterly, her beautiful eyes still full of tears, "woe is my heritage! The brightness of each dawn jars upon me, showing me how gloomy life is, and how utterly hopeless and lonely is the sea of despair upon which I am drifting. I welcome each night with joy, because—because it brings me one day nearer—nearer to *death*."

"You are young and fair; you have joy and life around you. Surely you are joking?"

"No, m'sieur. Ah, you do not know!" she sighed. "If you were aware of my secret, you would, I assure you, not be surprised that, even though surrounded by friends, I desire to die."

"But it is so extraordinary!" I said, walking beside her and chatting as if we were old acquaintances. "Have you never tried to unburden yourself by confiding your secret to some friend?"

"*Dieu*! No. I—I dare not."

"Dare not?" I echoed. "Of what are you afraid?"

"Afraid?" she repeated in a strained voice, speaking like one in a dream, with her eyes fixed straight before her. "Yes, I—I am a wretched, miserable coward, because I fear the punishment."

"Is your crime of such a flagitious character, then?"

"My crime?" she cried, turning suddenly upon me with flashing eyes. "What—what do you know of my crime? What do you insinuate?"

"Nothing, mademoiselle," I answered, as politely as I could, though amazed at her sudden change of manner. "Your own strange words must be my excuse for inquisitiveness."

"Then let us change the subject. To you my private affairs can be of no concern whatever."

I was not prepared for this stinging rebuff. We passed the front of the Casino, strolling through the shady gardens facing the Concha, and when we had rested upon a convenient seat, pleasantly sheltered from the sun, she grew communicative again. While I had been telling her of my journey over the Pyrenees to Madrid, her grief had been succeeded by gaiety, and when I related some amusing *contretemps* that had befallen me at a wayside *posada* in the Sierra de Guara, she laughed lightly. At length at my request, she drew out a silver case, and, in exchange for my card, gave me one bearing the name "Doroteita d'Avendano."

Then, with an ingenuousness that enhanced her personal charms, she told me of herself, that she was the only daughter of the Count Miguel d'Avendano, who had represented Castillejo in the Senate, but who had died a year ago. The widowed Countess—who had been her companion on the previous night—had let their mansion in the Calle Ancha de San Bernardo at Madrid to a wealthy foreigner, and since that time her mother and herself had been travelling, spending the winter at Cannes, the spring at Seville, and coming to San Sebastian for a few weeks previous to going north to Paris. She pointed out their villa from where we sat, a great white house with a terrace in front, standing out against a background of foliage on the side of the hill overlooking the bay. The Count, her father, had, I knew, been one of the most celebrated of Spanish statesmen. Referring to many well-known personages at Court as her friends, her observations regarding their little idiosyncrasies were full of dry humour. With a versatility of narrative she told me many little anecdotes of the Queen-Regent and the infant monarch, the knowledge of which betrayed an intimacy with the domestic arrangements of the palace, and for fully an hour gossiped on pleasantly.

"And amid this life of gaiety and happiness I find you kneeling in yonder church, abandoned to melancholy!" I observed at length, half reproachfully.

The light died out of her face.

"True," she sighed. "Sometimes for an hour or so I manage to forget, but sooner or later the sorrow that overshadows my life recurs to me in all its hideous reality, and when I am alone it overwhelms me. To the world I am compelled to appear *chic*, happy, and thoughtless. Few, indeed, who know me are aware that my feigned laughter is but a bitter wail of lamentation, that beneath my smile lies a broken heart."

"And your lover? Was he faithless? What of him?"

"What of him!" she gasped hoarsely, rising from the seat with her hands clenched. "I—I know nothing of him," she added, with a strange look in her eyes.

She laughed a hollow laugh, and as she drew on her long *suede* gloves, the bells of San Vicente announced the noon.

"I have been out too long already," she added, hurriedly rising. "We must part."

"May I not accompany you towards your home?" I asked.

"No, m'sieur," she answered firmly, holding out her hand.

"And when shall we resume our chat?" I asked.

She hesitated, gazing away to the misty cliffs across the bay. I half feared she would refuse to meet me again.

"If you are not bored by my wretchedness and bad temper," she said at last, with a sad smile, "I will be here to-morrow morning, at eleven."

"I shall not fail to keep the appointment," I said, delighted. "Meanwhile try and forget your secret; try and be equally happy with those around you, and remember that at least you have one sympathiser, even though he is almost a stranger."

Tears welled in her beautiful eyes as I clasped her hand.

"Thank you," she said in a low voice, trembling with emotion. "I—I appreciate your sympathy. *Au revoir, m'sieur, sans adieu.*"

For an instant our eyes met, then, turning towards the Concha, she walked away, and was, a few seconds later, hidden by a bend in the path.

I strolled back to the Ezcurra, utterly mystified. Women's ways are as many and as devious as "luck's lines" on one's hand, but the Senorita Doroteita was an enigma. I was not one of those "minor lovers" whose petty passions could be caged in a triolet, for her marvellous beauty and exquisite grace now held me in fascination.

No solution of the political crisis presented itself. In those agitated and troublous times under which Spain was labouring, I was compelled to make a daily journey to Bayonne, a distance of thirty-four miles, in order to dispatch my telegram to London. The Carlists were active; the various political parties were holding conferences incessantly; in military circles dissatisfaction was being openly expressed, and there were sinister rumours of a projected *coup d'etat*. With Senor Canovas del Castillo, Senor Romero y Robledo, and Senor Navarro Reverter I had had short interviews, the substance of which had been transmitted to London; and spending the brilliant sunny mornings in strolling with my enchanting senorita, the afternoons in writing, and the evenings in travelling to and fro across the frontier, the days glided by, and I took no count of them. In the course of those charming morning rambles we had visited Los Pasajes and Monte Igueldo, we had strolled along the Paseo de Ategorrita, and ascended Monte Orgullo to enjoy the view of the Pyrenees, and each hour I spent with her increased my admiration. She had discarded the mantilla, and was always dressed in gowns and hats that were unmistakably from the Rue de la Paix. Patrician refinement was stamped upon every line of her handsome countenance, and her conversation was always bright, witty, and delightful. One day, while we were walking along the Paseo de Ategorrita, beside the sea, outside the town, I explained to her how, as a newspaper correspondent, I was exceedingly anxious to obtain reliable information regarding the situation, and the earliest intimation as to the formation of the new Cabinet.

Then, as she expressed herself interested in journalism, I related in reply to her questions some of my adventures in pursuit of news. She was, I found, quite an enthusiast in politics, for she gave a critical opinion upon the probable policy of the various parties, declaring that the day of revolutions by *pronunciamiento* had not gone by, adding emphatic arguments that would have done credit to any member of the Chamber. I told her of the details I had already sent to London describing the efforts of Senor Canovas del Castillo to form a new Cabinet; but, after hearing all I had ascertained regarding a probable solution of the crisis, she shook her head, and, laughing, said—

"I believe your information has somewhat misled you. Although the deadlock is even more serious than you anticipate, yet matters may be temporarily adjusted at any moment."

"And when they are, I shall, alas! be compelled to bid you adieu," I said sorrowfully. "The memory of these few bright, happy days will dwell always within me."

In silence she gazed for a few moments away upon the broad expanse of green sunlit sea. Then she exclaimed—

"And you will return to London—and—and—forget me!"

"No, never, Doroteita," I said passionately. "I shall always look upon these as the happiest hours of my life!"

Her breast rose and fell. As we walked together, I held her small, well-gloved hand in mine, breathing into her ear the tender passion that had overwhelmed me. I scarce know what words I uttered, but she heard me patiently in pensive silence until I had concluded. Then, withdrawing her hand slowly but firmly, she replied in a voice that betrayed emotion—

"No, no. Our relationship can never be closer than that of friends. Our lives lie so very, very far apart."

"Ah, I know!" I cried in disappointment, stopping and gazing straight into her great liquid eyes. "If I were wealthy, I might dare to ask for your hand. As it is, Doroteita—as it is, may I not entertain hope?"

Slowly and sadly she shook her head.

"But I love you."

"That I do not doubt," she said huskily, sighing heavily.

"You do not reciprocate my affection sufficiently," I hazarded.

"I did not say so," she replied quickly, raising her dark lashes for an instant. "Perhaps I may even love you with as fierce a passion as you yourself have betrayed. Yet, though that may be so, we can never marry—never!"

"May I not know the reason?" I asked.

"No," she answered, with her eyes fixed seaward. "Soon I shall die—then perhaps you will ascertain the truth. Until then, let us be friends, not lovers."

I was sorely puzzled, for the mystery was so tantalising. Times without number I sought by artfully concealed questions to penetrate it, but she frustrated every effort, and when we parted outside the Casino at noon, my bewitching senorita grasped my hand in farewell, saying—

"We are true friends. Let us trust each other."

"We do," I answered, bending with reverence over the hand I held. "Our friendship will, I hope, last always—always."

Her heart seemed too full for further words, for her luminous eyes were filled with tears as she disengaged her hand and turned slowly away with uneven steps.

Again and again we met, but on each occasion I spoke of love, she requested me kindly but firmly to refrain from discussing the subject.

"It is enough," she said, one morning, while we were strolling in the Calle Santa Catalina—"enough that, in idling away a few hours each morning, we do not bore each other. Let us live for the present, enjoying to the full the few pleasant rambles that remain to us. Then, when we have parted, only pleasant memories will remain."

Sometimes I met her driving in the afternoon, or walking along the Concha in the evening with the Countess. Then she would smile a graceful recognition, but, being only a chance acquaintance, I was not introduced, neither was I invited to the Villa Guipuzcoa.

Late one afternoon, a fortnight after our first meeting, I returned to the Ezcurra from a long walk, having parted from her as usual, outside the Casino, when Senor Cos Gayon, a well-known member of the Senate, told me that Senor Canovas del Castillo had that morning had an audience of the Queen-Regent, and had at last undertaken to form a new Cabinet. This was an important piece of intelligence, inasmuch as it showed that the Conservatives would again hold office, and that, the loyalty of the military thus being assured, all fear of revolutionary troubles was at an end. Having spent an hour chatting with half a dozen politicians staying at the hotel, I ascended to my room to write a long dispatch descriptive of the situation.

The afternoon seemed too bright and balmy for work, therefore, before sitting down to my correspondence, I went out upon the balcony, and there smoked and dreamed until the shadows lengthened and over the broad waters of the Bay of Biscay there hung a glorious golden haze. A cool wind at last sprang up, and, returning into my room, I sat down and commenced to pen the latest intelligence for publication in London on the following morning. After writing about a quarter of an hour, voices in the adjoining room attracted my attention. Then suddenly I remembered that it was the Conservative leader's sitting-room. With the names of well-known politicians falling upon my ear, I crept noiselessly across the polished floor to the locked door that divided the two apartments. Then, placing my ear close against the door, I stood on the alert.

My heart beat quickly, for in a few moments I ascertained that a meeting was in progress to decide upon the formation of the Cabinet. I recognised the voice of Senor Canovas, who acted as president, and there must have been fully eighteen or twenty of the most prominent members of his party present. With paper and pencil in hand, I listened to the discussion, as each name was submitted for the eight principal offices of State, Senor Canovas himself being, of course, President of the Council. The first business was the acceptance of the chief of the Ministry of Foreign Affairs by the Duke of Tetuan, and it was agreed without a single dissentient that Senor Romero y Robledo should become Minister of Justice. Senor Bosch and Senor Castellanos accepted office as Ministers of Public Works and the Colonies respectively; but a discussion lasting nearly an hour took place regarding the Ministry of Finance, until an agreement was at length arrived at that to Senor Navarro Reverter the portfolio should again be allotted. Protracted discussions also ensued regarding the appointment of the Ministers of Marine, War, and the Interior, and it was not until nearly seven that these appointments were made. Then Senor Canovas read a complete list of the newly-formed Cabinet,—each member of which was present, and expressed his acceptance of office,—afterwards stating that the crisis was at an end, and that at noon on the following day he had arranged to place the list in the hands of the Queen-Regent.

Little did the President of the Council dream that the list he had read out had been carefully noted by an eavesdropping journalist, and that even while his colleagues were congratulating each other upon the amicable solution of the crisis, the correspondent was busy preparing a list of the new Cabinet, which would be published in London in the morning, and known throughout England many hours before it became public in Spain.

Congratulating myself upon my good fortune, I finished my dispatch, waited until all the politicians had left the President's room, and then descended to the *table d'hote*. Opposite me sat Senor Romero y Robledo, the new Minister of Justice, but in reply to my carefully-veiled inquiries he gave no sign that a Cabinet had been formed. The decision was, I knew, a profound secret until the Queen had given her assent. While idling over dessert, with just an hour to catch my train to Bayonne, the waitress handed me a note, stating that a man-servant awaited a reply.

On the envelope was a great gilt crest, and the address was written in an unfamiliar angular hand. As I tore it open, a breath of sweet perfume greeted my nostrils, and the words I read in French were as follows:—

Villa Guipuzcoa, *July 22*

"My brother Luis has returned unexpectedly front Cuba, and mamma and I are leaving with him for Madrid by the mail to-night. Will you not call here to wish me farewell; or shall we never meet again? Give bearer a verbal reply, and come at once if possible.

Doroteita

With satisfaction I recognised that it gave an opportunity for an introduction to her family, yet I was nevertheless doubtful about being able to get to Bayonne. Having, however, glanced at the time-table, and ascertained that there was another train at a quarter-past nine, by which I could get over the frontier at midnight, and finding I should be able to spend about an hour at the villa, I decided to respond to the invitation, and gave the girl an answer to that effect. Several times I read the brief, sweetly-scented note, then, finishing my wine, I rose, and, after a "brush up," entered a cab and told the man my destination.

As I alighted before the great handsome house on the hillside overlooking the bay, the door was thrown open by a servant in livery, who conducted me across a wide square hall, in which a fountain was playing, and ushered me into a small but luxuriously-furnished room.

Taking my card upon a salver, the man returned almost immediately, saying—

"The Senorita Doroteita will be with you in a few moments, Senor."

Then he withdrew, and almost before I had had an opportunity of inspecting the pretty room, which was evidently a boudoir, the door again opened and Doroteita entered.

"I'm so glad you have come," she exclaimed, with a bright smile of welcome, as she grasped both my hands. "I thought perhaps you would be compelled to go to Bayonne to-night."

"So I am," I said. "Nevertheless, I could not part from you without just one brief word of farewell."

Sinking into a low wicker chair, she motioned me to a seat beside her, and told me how her brother, an army officer, who had been for four years in Cuba, had returned that afternoon, and the Countess, on account of some family matters, had resolved to accompany him to Madrid, where he was compelled to report himself on the morrow. She looked absolutely bewitching in a low-necked gown of some dove-grey clinging material, that disclosed her delicately-moulded chest and arms, while in her blue-black hair was a single crimson flower that gave the touch of colour necessary for artistic effect. It was a blossom I had never before seen, almost waxen, and similar to a camellia, but larger and of richer colour.

When we had been chatting some time, each expressing regret that the hour of parting had come, and hope that we should meet again ere long, she suddenly asked—

"Is it absolutely imperative that you should cross the frontier to-night? We go by the Sud Express at eleven-fifteen, why not remain and see us off?"

"I cannot, Doroteita," I replied. "It is most important that I should go to Bayonne to-night—for the last time."

"Then the crisis is ended?" she exclaimed, suddenly interested. "Has a new Ministry been formed?"

"Yes," I replied. "My work is finished."

Her brows contracted for a second as if a sudden thought had occurred to her; then she shivered slightly, and, rising, crossed the room, and, drawing the heavy silken curtains across the window, shut out the extensive view of the moonlit bay.

"Our wanderings have been so pleasant and unconventional that I am loth to leave," she said, as she slowly sank again among her cushions. "Nevertheless, I hope some day before long to be in London. Then perhaps we shall be able to spend a few more pleasant hours together."

"I hope so," I said earnestly, rising and taking her hand. "I must, alas! go, or I shall not catch my train."

But she would not hear of my departure, declaring that by the road on the other side of the hill I could reach the station in ten minutes, and, assuring me that she would send one of the servants with me as guide, urged me to resume my seat. Just as I was about to do so, there entered a tall slim man about thirty-five, wearing the uniform of a cavalry officer, and my pretty hostess, rising, introduced him as Luis, her brother.

He was a good-looking fellow, dark and sun-tanned, but when he smiled, cynicism lurked in the corners of his mouth, and instinctively I disliked him. Not that he was supercilious—on the contrary, his greeting was quite effusive. He declared himself much attached to his sister, and any friend of hers was likewise his friend. He regretted that he had to leave for Madrid, but military orders could not be disobeyed. Together we sat chatting, Doroteita ordering some wine, which was served almost immediately by the man who had admitted me. Luis d'Avendano proved a brilliant conversationalist and entertaining companion, but somehow I could not help regarding him with a curious indescribable suspicion. Once I caught the pair exchanging significant glances, and this increased my vague mistrust. Yet his sister lolled in her chair, with a great cushion of yellow silk behind her head, fanning herself slowly, and chatting with that light coquetry that had so charmed me.

A little clock chiming on its silver bells caused me to spring to my feet.

"Nine o'clock!" I exclaimed. "You must excuse me, otherwise I really shall not catch my train."

"Must you go?" asked Doroteita, in a tone of regret, closing her fan with a snap and rising also.

"Yes," I said. "This is my last train. I must wish you *au revoir*, in the hope that we may meet again at a date not far distant."

"Aren't you going to exchange tokens of friendship?" Luis suggested, laughing in his careless, good-humoured way. "Give my future brother-in-law your flower, Doroteita."

She laughed and blushed, then taking the crimson blossom from her hair, handed it to me. I was about to inhale its fragrance when the strange, fixed look in her eyes fascinated me, and as I placed it in the lapel of my coat with a murmured word of thanks, I confess I was startled by the sudden transformation of her countenance.

"Good-bye," I said, taking her hand.

It was cold, limp, and trembling.

"Adieu," she answered huskily.

I turned to shake hands with her brother, but before I could do so, he had pounced upon me from behind, holding my arms powerless, crying—

"No, no, my friend, you will not escape so easily!"

"What—what do you mean?" I gasped in abject amazement.

"I mean that you do not leave this place alive," he hissed in my ear. Though I could not see him, I could feel his hot breath upon my cheek, and struggled violently to free myself, but in his iron grip I seemed powerless as a child.

"Now, quick, Doroteita!" he commanded. "Remember, we have no time to lose. Don't stand staring there!"

"Do you mean to kill me?" I cried, clenching my teeth and struggling with all my might to free my arms.

"Curse you, woman! Don't you hear me?" he yelled at Doroteita, who stood transfixed, with face ashen pale and hands clenched in desperation. "Remember what we have at stake! You have trapped him—finish your work, or—or I'll kill *you*!"

In a second she sprang forward, and, snatching from my buttonhole the flower she had given me, held her handkerchief over my mouth with one hand, while with the other she pressed the flower against my nostrils. It seemed damp with some evil-smelling fluid, and though I struggled, she held my face with such determined force, that the leaves of the blossom were forced into my nose, and I was compelled to inhale the disagreeable perfume they emitted.

The odour was strange, and in a few seconds produced a curious giddiness such as I had never before experienced. My brain became paralysed and my limbs assumed an unaccountable rigidness. I tried to speak, but was unable. My jaws seemed to have become suddenly fixed, as if attacked by tetanus. A thrill of horror ran through me, for I could not breathe, and the pang of pain that shot through my eyes was excruciating.

Feeling myself utterly helpless in the hands of those who had so cunningly plotted my murder, I wondered in that brief instant whether Luis was Doroteita's lover, and whether on discovering our friendship, he had planned this terrible and merciless revenge. My enchantress's handsome face, now hideously distorted by mingled fear and passion, was close to me, her eyes riveted to mine, and as she pressed the strange flower against my face, her white lips moved as if speaking to me. But I was deaf. My senses had been destroyed.

Next second, though I fought against the sudden faintness that crept over me, my head swam, and my surroundings grew indistinct. I felt myself falling. Then, by a sudden darkness that fell upon me, the present became blotted out.

On opening my aching eyes, they became dazzled by a bar of golden sunlight that strayed in between the closed curtains.

Amazed, I gazed around from where I lay stretched upon the floor. Then, in a few moments, the recollection of the strange events of the previous night returned to me in all their grim reality. The woman I had adored had, from some motive utterly incomprehensible, enticed me there to murder me! Feeling terribly weak and ill, I managed to struggle to my feet. I looked for the fatal flower, but could not find it. Then my eyes fell upon the clock, and I was amazed to discover it was past three in the afternoon.

I had remained unconscious nearly eighteen hours!

Half fearful lest another attempt should be made upon me, I searched the rooms on the ground floor and shouted. No one stirred. The house was tenantless!

Walking with difficulty down the hill towards the Ezcurra, I suddenly remembered my dispatch, and placing my hand in the inner pocket of my coat, I found it gone! It had evidently been stolen; but for what object was an enigma.

As I passed onward under the trees of the Calle del Pozzo, boys were crying *La Voz*, and from their strident shouts, and the eagerness of purchasers, I knew that the new Ministry had been officially announced. My intellect seemed too disordered to think, so I merely returned to the hotel, and, casting myself on the bed, slept till next morning.

I refrained from lodging a complaint with the police, believing that my extraordinary story would be discredited; nevertheless, I remained three days longer, endeavouring to discover some facts regarding the Countess d'Avendano and her daughter. All I could glean was, that, a month before, they had taken the Villa Guipuzcoa for the season, and that a number of tradespeople, including two jewellers, were now exceedingly anxious to ascertain their whereabouts. Therefore, after much futile effort to ascertain the truth about Doroteita, I at length returned to London, being compelled to invent an absurdly lame excuse for not telegraphing the information of the new Cabinet.

Last July I again found myself in Spain. Another serious crisis had occurred. The Carlists were known to be carrying on an active propaganda, and I had been despatched to Madrid, so as to be on the spot if serious trouble arose. Only one London newspaper keeps a resident correspondent in the Spanish capital, the remainder of the news from that city being supplied through a well-known agency. A few days after my arrival at the Hotel de Rome, in the Caballero de Gracia, I called upon Senor Navarro Reverter, Minister of Finance, and was granted an interview. I desired to ascertain his views on the situation, and as he had been very communicative during those stormy times at San Sebastian a year before, I had no doubt that he would give me a few opinions worth telegraphing.

As I entered his cosy private room in the Calle de Alcala, and he rose to greet me, my gaze became fixed upon the mantelshelf behind him, for upon it stood two cabinet photographs of a man and a woman.

The one was a counterfeit presentment of Luis d'Avendano; the other a portrait of Doroteita!

When I had formally "interviewed" him upon the financial reforms and other matters regarding which I desired his opinion, I asked to be allowed to see the photographs, and he handed them to me with a smile.

"Doroteita d'Avendano!" I exclaimed. The features were unmistakable, though the dress was different.

"Are they—er—friends of yours?" the Minister asked, regarding me keenly from beneath his shaggy brows.

"They were—once," I answered. "Ever since we were at San Sebastian last year I have been endeavouring to trace them."

"What? Did she add you to her list of victims?" he asked, laughing.

"Well, the plot was scarcely successful, otherwise I should not be here now," I replied. Then I told him briefly how, after luring me to their villa, the interesting pair had attempted to murder me.

"Extraordinary!" he exclaimed, when I had finished. "Curiously enough, however, your story supplies just the link in the chain of evidence that was missing at their trial."

"Their trial?" I exclaimed. "Tell me about them."

"Well, in the first place, the enchantress you knew as Doroteita d'Avendano was none other than the notorious Liseta Gonzalez, known to the police as 'The Golden Hand.'"

"'The Golden Hand'?" I echoed in amazement. I had heard much of the extraordinary career of an adventuress bearing that *sobriquet*; how she had moved in the best society in Paris and Vienna, and how in the latter city, in a single year, in her character as queen of the *demi-monde*, she had spent 50,000 pounds, the money of her dupes. Indeed, her adventures had been the talk of Europe.

"Yes," he continued, smiling at my astonishment. "No doubt you have read in your English newspapers all about the many ingenious frauds she has perpetrated. For the past five years she has been well-known in various characters in Pau, Rome, Paris, and Vienna; her schemes have invariably been successful, and her escape from the police has been accomplished just at the right moment, in a manner almost incredible. But the audacious boldness of a *coup* she effected a year ago caused her downfall."

"A year ago?" I said. "Was it during the time I knew her?"

"Yes. While spending the summer at San Sebastian with Mateo Sanchez,—a Bourse adventurer of Madrid, who, under the name of Luis d'Avendano, passed as her brother,—she conceived, during the Cabinet crisis, a very ingenious scheme for gigantic operations on the Bourse with certain success. The circumstances were remarkable, and your story supplies the facts which have remained until now a mystery. Unaware of the true character of Sanchez, I had employed him as agent in various transactions shortly before the crisis, and he had thus become aware of my intentions to institute certain financial reforms that would affect the Bourse to a considerable extent. 'The Golden Hand,' it appears, with her usual shrewdness, pointed out how the knowledge thus acquired would enable him to operate with success, if only he could be certain of my reappointment as Finance Minister, and the pair forthwith carried into effect an ingeniously arranged plan. Apparently you were watched, and, it having been ascertained that, as correspondent of an influential journal, you were a likely person to obtain the very earliest intimation of the formation of the Cabinet, they laid their plans to entrap you."

"I confess I little dreamed of foul play when I entered the Villa Guipuzcoa," I observed.

"At the trial it was a mystery how they obtained knowledge of the State secret," he continued. "But it is now quite plain that on the evening when the portfolios were arranged, they, being aware of the devices to which you would probably resort in order to obtain accurate information, enticed you to their house, and then, having ascertained from your own lips that the Ministry had been formed, resolved to carry out their cunningly-devised scheme. They saw that you were the only member of the public who knew the secret, and if they prevented you from despatching it to London,—whence it was certain to be re-telegraphed here,—it would give them time to get to Madrid on the following morning and operate on the Bourse some hours before the announcement of the new Ministry."

"She seemed so ingenuous and charming, that I suspected nothing—until—"

"Until she attempted to murder you—eh?" he said, taking up her portrait, and gazing upon it with a smile. "To say the least, the plot was a most extraordinary one. By your admission that the crisis was at an end, they knew you held a list of the new Ministers, and as you persisted in your endeavour to catch the train to the frontier, it became necessary for them to possess themselves of the list, and silence you, in order to escape to Madrid, and on the opening of the Bourse next day purchase the stock which they knew would rise immediately the official announcement was published. 'The Golden Hand' gave you as a souvenir the flower she wore, in the expectation that you would inhale its fatal perfume, as other victims had done."

"It was very similar to a camellia," I said. "Has anything been ascertained regarding it?"

"Oh yes. The flower she sometimes wore in her hair, and which appeared rather like a camellia, was at the trial proved to be the Kali Mujah, or death-rose of Sumatra, which is so deadly that its perfume is sufficient to cause unconsciousness, and sometimes even death. It was found that she actually cultivated these flowers, and that on more than one occasion she had used them upon her victims with fatal result. She gave one to you, but you merely placed it in your buttonhole; therefore, just as you were about to depart, her lover gripped you, while she pressed the fatal blossom into your nostrils. Then you lapsed into unconsciousness, and half an hour afterwards the enterprising pair were on their way to Madrid, where, on the following morning, they purchased a quantity of stock, with money secured by your idol Doroteita from one of her dupes, the Comte de Segonnaux, whose death had been caused by the poisonous blossom in a similar manner to the attempt upon yourself."

"Were their operations on the Bourse successful?" I asked.

"Entirely so. Unaware of these events, I put forward my financial scheme in the Chamber a month afterwards, with the result that the stock they had secured rose to unparalleled prices, and then they effected a gigantic *coup*, gaining nearly a million pesetas. But the boldness of the scheme caused their downfall, for the colossal extent of their transactions attracted the attention of the police, the result being that eventually the murder of the Comte de Segonnaux at Toledo was conclusively proved, and your divinity's identity with 'The Golden Hand' fully established."

"Were they both tried?" I asked, amazed at his extraordinary story.

"Yes. Mateo Sanchez was found guilty of being an accessory in the assassination of the Comte, and sentenced at the last sitting of the Assize Court to fifteen years' imprisonment; while the bewitching Liseta, condemned for the murder, is at present serving a life sentence at the convict prison at Barcelona."

A quarter of an hour later I had wished my genial friend the Minister adieu, and, full of grave reflections, crossed the sunlit Puerta del Sol, carrying in my pocket, as a souvenir of a foolish infatuation, the portrait of "The Golden Hand."

III

The Masked Circe

The success of "The Masked Circe" in last year's Royal Academy was incontestable, not only for the intrinsic beauty of the picture, but from the fact that the personal charms of a handsome woman were perpetuated without compromising her features. Woman's vanity often outruns her natural diffidence, and the consciousness of her great beauty stifles the conscience of modesty.

Visitors to the Academy know the picture. Circe, seated on a throne, with her back to a great circular mirror, presents a half-draped figure of marvellous delicate colouring and beauty of outline. One hand holds aloft a golden wine-goblet, and the other a tapering wand, while upon the tesselated pavement before the dais purple grapes and yellow roses have been strewn. The black hair of the daughter of Perseis falls in profusion about her bare shoulders, and strays over her breast, but her features are hidden by a half-mask of black silk. The lips, with their *arc de cupidon*, are slightly parted, disclosing an even row of pearly teeth, and giving an expression of reckless *diablerie*.

Of the thousands who have gazed upon it in admiration, none knows the somewhat remarkable story connected with it. As I have been closely associated with it, from the day it was outlined in charcoal, until the evening it was packed in a crate and sent for the inspection of the hanging committee, it is perhaps *apropos* that I should relate the narrative.

The studio of my old friend, Dick Carruthers, the man who painted it, is on Campden Hill, Kensington, within a few hundred yards of where I reside, and in the centre of an aesthetic artistic colony. We have been chums for years, for on many occasions he has displayed his talent as a black and white artist in illustrating my articles and stories in various magazines. He is a popular painter, and as handsome a man as ever had a picture "on the line."

Three years ago, when the prologue of this secret drama was enacted, he was in the habit of coming over when the light had faded, to smoke a cigarette and discuss art and literature with me. I was glad of a chat after a hard day's work at my writing-table, but his companionship had one drawback. He drivelled over a girl he loved, and was forever suggesting that I might take her as a character and drag her into the novel upon which I was engaged.

One day he drew a cabinet photograph carefully from his pocket, and placed it upon the blotting-pad before me.

The girl he loved! Bah! I knew her, though I did not tell him so. She was a dark-haired, pink-and-white beauty that flitted through artistic Bohemia like a butterfly in a hothouse. The sight of the pictured face brought back to me the memory of days long past—of a closed chapter in my life's history. I remembered the first time I saw Ethel Broughton, fully five years before. She wore a soiled pink wrapper, her satin slippers were trodden down at heel, and she had a bottle of champagne at her elbow. At that time her lover, grandiloquent and impecunious Mr. Harry Oranmore, a bad but handsome actor, had been untrue to her, and she, a third-rate actress, who had an *ingenue* part at a Strand theatre, was reviling him. I had been taken to her house and introduced by a mutual friend, but she scarcely heeded me. Probably she was thinking of Oranmore, for she clasped her slim fingers round her suffering throat, and offered up an occasional sob, following it with a silent but protracted draught from her glass.

The result of this interview was but natural. Dazzled by her beauty, I sympathised with her, endeavoured to cheer her, and concluded by falling violently in love with her. At that time I was writing numbers of dramatic criticisms, and I confess I used what weight my opinions possessed for the purpose of her advancement. It is needless to refer to the smooth and uninterrupted course of our love. Suffice it to say that we were both Bohemians, and that within a year I had the satisfaction of sitting before the footlights, watching her make her debut as "leading lady" at a West End theatre, and a few days later of observing her photograph exhibited in shop windows among those of other stage beauties.

But, alas! those halcyon days were all too brief. Suddenly the scales fell from my eyes. A scene occurred between us—and we parted.

To think that sin should lie for years in the blood, just as arsenic does in a corpse!

When I discovered that Dick Carruthers was wasting the very honest and ardent emotions of his heart at this feverish fairy's shrine, I resolved to take him aside, and, without admitting that I knew her, give him a verbal drubbing. I did so, but he bit his moustache fiercely, and turned upon me.

"She is charming," he said, "and I love her."

"Ah! I know the type—"

"You know nothing, old fellow!" he exclaimed, flushing angrily. "But"—he shrugged his shoulders—"the prejudices of the world count for—what? Nothing at all. The curse of the Philistine is his Philistinism."

"Very well, Dick, old chap, forget my words," I said. "I approach your idol in the properly reverential spirit."

"You shall see her before long." His gaze grew bright, soft, and vague, as one who catches glimpses of the floating garments of supernatural mysteries. "Ah, she is lovely! Only an artist can appreciate her beauty."

I saw that words were of no avail. Like Ulysses, he was living in the paradise of Aeaea, heedless of everything under the spell she had cast about him.

One night, not long after I had expressed my sentiments to him regarding his infatuation, I entered his studio, and found his goddess seated by the fire, with her shapely feet upon the fender, sipping kummel from a tiny glass, and holding a lighted cigarette between her dainty fingers.

Dick flung down his palette, and came forward to introduce me. Her dark eyes met mine, and we tacitly agreed not to recognise each other, therefore we bowed as perfect strangers. As I seated myself, and she poured me out a liqueur, I caught her glancing furtively at me under her long lashes. She had grown even handsomer than when last I had seen her, and was the picture of the romantic *Bohemienne*. Her dress was of black gauze, through which the milky whiteness of her figure seemed to shine. Yet, as she turned her beautiful face towards me, I was struck by the complete effect of physical and moral frailty that she presented.

She expressed pleasure at meeting me, remarking that she had read my last novel, and had been keenly interested in it.

When I had briefly acknowledged the compliment she paid me, she said—

"One thing always strikes me in reading your stories. Your women are inevitably false and fickle. Perhaps, however, you write from personal experience of the failings of my sex," she laughed.

Glancing sharply at her, I saw that her eyes did not waver.

"It is true I once knew a woman who proved false and infamous," I replied, with some emphasis.

"And you avenge yourself by reviling all of us. It is really too bad!" she said, pouting like a spoiled child.

"By Jove, old fellow," Dick chimed in, "do tell us about your romance! It would be interesting to know the reason you set your face against all the fair ones."

But I succeeded in turning the conversation into another channel. I saw I had intruded upon them, so, making an excuse, I bade them *au revoir*, and returned to my own book-lined den.

Unlocking a drawer in my writing-table, I took out a packet of letters that still emitted a stale odour of violets. Then I lit my pipe, and one by one read them through, pausing and pondering over the declarations of passionate love they contained. Far into the night I sat reviewing the romance of bygone days, until I came to the last letter. It was a cold, formal note, merely a few lines of hurried scrawl, and read: "You are right. I have been false to you. Think no more of me. By the time you receive this I shall be on my way to New York; nevertheless, you will be always remembered by yours unworthily—Ethel." Bitter memories of the past overwhelmed me; but at last, growing impatient, and tossing the letters back into the drawer, I strove to forget. The clock had struck two, and my reading-lamp was burning low and sputtering when I rose to retire for the night. I confess that my frame of mind surprised me, inasmuch as I actually found myself still loving her.

"Good afternoon. I hope I don't disturb you."

Looking up from my work, I saw Ethel.

"Not at all. Pray sit down," I said coldly, motioning her to an armchair. "To what do I owe the honour of this visit?"

She pulled off her long gloves, and let her sealskin cape fall at her feet, while I put down my pen, and, rising, stood with my back to the fire.

With her she had brought the odour of violets, the same that I remembered years ago; the same perfume that always stirred sad memories within me.

"You don't welcome me very warmly," she said in a disappointed tone, as she grasped my hand, and looked steadily into my eyes.

"No," I said sternly. "Last night I told you that a woman had embittered my life. The woman I referred to was yourself."

"Ah," she said, striving to suppress a sob, "Forgive me! I—I was mad then. I loved you; but I did not apprehend the consequence."

"Love? What nonsense to speak of it, when through your baseness I have been almost ruined. Think of your actions on the day before you left me; how you took from that drawer a signed blank cheque, with which you drew six hundred pounds,—nearly all the money I possessed,—and then fled with your lover. Is that the way a woman shows her affection?"

Her head was bowed in humiliation.

"Forgive me, Harold," she said, with intense earnestness. "I admit that I wronged you cruelly, that I discarded the honest love you gave me; but you—you do not know how weak we women are when temptation is in our path. Cannot I now make amends?"

I shook my head sadly.

"Don't say that you will not forgive," she implored tearfully. "At least I am honest. My object in coming this afternoon was to repay the money I—I borrowed." And she drew forth an envelope from her pocket and handed it to me.

"There are notes for six hundred pounds," she added, as I took it and felt the crisp paper inside.

"How did you obtain it?" I asked, hesitating to receive it.

"I have earned it honestly, every penny," she replied. "Since we parted, I have become popular in America, and played 'lead' in nearly all the great cities. During the years that have gone I have many, many times wondered what had become of you, for in your writings I read plainly how soured and embittered you had become."

"And where is Oranmore?"

"Dead. He contracted typhoid while we were playing in San Francisco, and it terminated fatally."

"Ethel," I said gravely, taking her hand in mine, "you have fascinated Dick Carruthers, my friend; and you will treat him as you treated me."

"No, no. I love him," she said in a fierce half-whisper, adding, "Keep secret the fact that we loved one another, and I swear before Heaven I will be true to him. If he marries me, he shall never have cause for regret—never!"

"Suppose I told him? What would he think of you?"

"You will not!" she cried, clinging to me. "You are too honourable for that. Promise to keep my secret!"

"For the present I will preserve silence," I answered, my heart softening towards her. "But I cannot promise that I will never tell him."

"I am going to sit to him as model," she said, after a brief silence. "What character do you think would best suit me?"

"Well, I should suggest that of Circe—the woman who broke men's hearts," I replied, mischievously.

"Excellent! I shall be able to assume that character well," she said, with a grim smile. "I will tell him."

Spring came and went, but I saw very little of Dick. He had received a commission from one of the illustrated papers to make a series of sketches of scenery in Scotland, and consequently he was away a good deal. Whenever he paid flying visits to London, however, he always looked me up, but, strangely enough, never mentioned Ethel. Nevertheless, I ascertained that they frequently met.

At the close of a blue summer's day, when the dreamy, golden haze wrapped the city in a mystic charm, I called at the studio, having heard that he had returned, and was settling down to work.

When I entered, Dick was standing before his easel, pipe in mouth and crayon in hand, busily sketching; while on the raised "throne" before him sat Ethel, radiant and beautiful. A tender smile played about her lips. It seemed as though a happiness—full, complete, perfectly satisfying—had taken possession of her, and lifted her out of herself—out of the world even.

"Welcome, old fellow!" Dick cried, turning to shake hands with me. "Behold my Circe!" and he waved his hand in the direction of his model. "Ethel will not sit for any other subject. It hardly does her justice—does it?"

"It is a strange fancy of mine," she explained, when I had greeted her. "I'm sure the dress is very becoming—isn't it?" And she waved the goblet she was holding above her head.

"Your pose is perfect, dear. Please don't alter it," urged the artist; who, advancing to his easel again, continued the free, rapid outline.

We chatted and laughed together for nearly an hour, until the tints of pearl and rose had melted imperceptibly into the deep night sky; then Dick lit the lamps, while Ethel retired into the model's sanctum to resume her nineteenth century attire.

Presently she reappeared, and we went to dine together at a restaurant in Piccadilly, afterwards visiting a theatre, and spending a very pleasant evening.

Poor Dick! I was sorry that he was so infatuated. He was such a large-hearted, honest fellow, that I felt quite pained when I anticipated the awakening that must inevitably come sooner or later. He knew absolutely nothing of her past, and was quite ignorant that she had been a popular actress.

In the months that followed, I visited the studio almost daily, and watched the growth of the picture. Dick was putting his whole soul into the composition, and my knowledge of art—acquired by years of idling in the ateliers of the Quartier Latin, and dabbling with the colours a little myself—told me that he was engaged upon what promised to be his finest work.

The face was a lifelike portrait. The delicate tints of the neck and arms were reproduced with a skill that betrayed the master hand, and the reflection in the mirror behind had a wonderfully natural appearance, while the bright colours enhanced the general effect of gay, reckless abandon.

The fair model herself was charmed with it. Woman's vanity always betrays itself over her picture.

One evening, at the time the canvas was receiving its finishing touches, I returned home from a stroll across Kensington Gardens, and, on going in, heard some one playing upon my piano, and a sweet soprano voice singing Trotere's "In Old Madrid." I recognised the clear tones as those of Ethel.

"Ah, Harold!" she cried, jumping up as I entered the room. "I was amusing myself until your return. I—I have something to tell you."

"Well, what is it?" I asked, rather surprised.

"Cannot you guess? Dick has asked me to become his wife," she said in a low tone.

"The thing's impossible!" I cried warmly. "I will not allow it. You may be friends, but he shall never marry you."

"How cruel you are!" she said, with a touch of sadness. "But, after all, your apprehensions are groundless. I have refused."

"Refused? Why?"

"For reasons of my own," she replied in a harsh, strained voice. "If—if he speaks to you, urge him to abandon thoughts of love, and regard me as a friend only."

"You are at least sensible, Ethel," I said. "It is gratifying to know that you recognise the impossibility of such an union."

Tears welled in her eyes. She nodded, but did not reply.

A DRY, GREY DAY IN March. It was "Show Sunday," that institution in the art world, when the painter opens his studio to his friends and the public, to show them the picture he is about to send to the Academy. The exhibition is in many instances but the showing beforehand of the garlands of victory in a battle which is doomed to be lost, for when the opening day comes, many of the anxious artists do not have the luck to see their pictures hung at all. Then insincere admirers smile in their sleeves at the painter's chagrin. I have always been thankful that the happy writer of books has no such ordeal to face. He never reads his new romance to his friends, nor do his well-wishers applaud in advance. Reviewers have first tilt at "advance copies," and very properly.

From morn till eve on "Show Sunday," Campden Hill is always blocked by the carriages of the curious, and studios are besieged by fashionable crowds, whose chatter and laughter mingles pleasantly with the clinking of tea-cups. On this occasion, as on previous ones, I assisted Dick to receive his visitors, but unfortunately Ethel had been taken suddenly unwell, and could not attend.

My anticipations proved correct. "Circe" was voted an unqualified success. The opinions of critics who dropped in were unanimous that it was the artist's masterpiece, and that the expression and general conception were marvellous—a verdict endorsed by gushing society women, bored club men, and the inane *jeunesse doree*.

A scrap of conversation I overheard in the course of the afternoon, however, caused me to ponder.

An elderly man, evidently a foreigner, wearing the violet ribbon of the French Academy in his buttonhole, was standing with a young girl in the crowd around the easel.

"Why, look, papa! That face!" the girl cried, when her eyes fell upon the canvas. "It is *her* portrait! Surely the Signore cannot know!"

"*Dio!*" exclaimed the old man, evidently recognising the features. "The picture is indeed magnificent; but to think that she should allow herself to appear in that character! Come away, Zelie; let us go."

I heard no more, for they turned and left. Having acted as eavesdropper, I could hardly question them. Nevertheless, I was sorely puzzled.

"Look! Read that!"

In surprise I glanced up from my work of romance-weaving on the following morning, and saw Dick, pale and agitated, standing at my elbow.

The letter he placed before me was in a woman's hand, and emitted the faintest breath of violets. A glance was sufficient to recognise that the sprawly writing was Ethel's.

Taking it up, I eagerly read the following lines it contained:—

Dear Dick,

I regret to tell you that circumstances preclude me from ever meeting you again. I am going far away, where you cannot find me. It was foolish for us to have loved, therefore forget me. That you may meet some one far worthier than myself, and that 'Circe' may bring you fame and fortune, is the most sincere hope of your models.

Ethel

"I warned you against your infatuation, old fellow," I said seriously.

"But I couldn't help it. I—I loved her," he answered in a hoarse, trembling voice.

"Forget her," I argued. "She is worthless and vain; why make yourself miserable?"

"Ah, you are right!" he said, as if suddenly impressed by the force of my arguments, while his face assumed a hard, determined expression. "She is Circe indeed, and she had her foot upon my neck. But it is all over," he added bitterly. "I shall think no more of her."

Then he wished me an abrupt farewell, and left, apparently in order to conceal his emotion.

That evening I called at Dick's house, but was informed by his housekeeper that he had packed his bag and departed, stating that he would not return for at least a month, perhaps longer. When I entered the studio, gloomy in the twilight, I was astonished to find that the "Circe" had been removed from the easel, and that it was standing in a corner with its face to the wall.

Something prompted me to turn it, and when I did so, I discovered to my dismay that in his frenzy of mad despair he had taken a brushful of black paint and drawn it across the face, making a great, ugly, disfiguring daub over the forehead and eyebrows, utterly ruining the features, and producing a curiously forbidding effect.

The colour was not dry, therefore I was enabled to remove the greater portion of it with a silk handkerchief, but I saw with regret that the tints of the forehead had been irretrievably ruined, rendering the picture valueless.

The days went by. The limit for sending in to the Academy was approaching; but Dick did not write, and I could only wonder vaguely where he was wandering. It was a great pity, I thought, that such a fine work should not be exhibited. Yet the wilful obliteration had utterly spoiled it.

While sitting in his studio musing one day, it suddenly occurred to me that if the flaw upon the forehead could be hidden, it might, after all, be sent for the inspection of the hanging committee.

Taking it up, I examined it minutely in the light. The idea of placing a half-mask upon the face suggested itself, and without delay I proceeded to carry it into effect. The little skill with the brush that I possess enabled me to paint in the half-lights upon the black silk, and the laughing eyes being fortunately intact, I allowed them to peer through the apertures.

The effect produced was startling, and none could have been more astonished at the result of my daubing than myself. The mask seemed to increase the reckless *diablerie* of its wearer, and enhance the fairness of the complexion, while it added an air of mystery not at all unpleasing to the eye.

A few days later, I dispatched it to the Academy, and waited patiently for the opening day, when I experienced the mingled surprise and satisfaction of seeing it hung "upon the line."

The "Masked Circe" was pronounced one of the pictures of the year. Thousands admired it. The papers were full of laudatory notices; but the man who painted it, unaware of the fame he had suddenly achieved, was hiding his sorrow somewhere in the Vosges. A stray copy of an English newspaper containing a notice of his work, which Dick picked up in a hotel, however, caused him to return.

He burst into my room unceremoniously one morning, still attired in his travelling ulster. I saw that he was haggard-eyed and wild-looking. From his conversation, I knew that time had not healed the wound in his heart.

"I shall never be able to thank you sufficiently, old chap, for touching up my daub. It seems that the public admire *her* as much as I have done. I—I shall find her some day; then she will return to me."

"Still thinking of her?" I observed reproachfully.

"Yes; always, always," he replied, shaking his head sorrowfully. "I—I cannot forget."

Dick's popularity steadily increased; lucrative commissions poured in upon him, and he settled down to such hard, methodical work, that I began to think he had forgotten the woman who had enmeshed him.

With beaming face he came to me one summer's morning and announced that, although the committee of the Chantrey Bequest had offered to purchase the "Masked Circe," he had just received a letter from the Count di Sestri, the well-known Anglo-Italian millionaire and art patron, saying that he desired to buy it, and asking him to go down to Oxted Park, his seat in Surrey, to arrange the price.

"I am going to-day," he said. "You masked her, and it is only fair that you should have a word in the bargain. You must come too."

At first I hesitated, but at length acquiesced.

That evening the Count received us in the library of his country mansion, and congratulated Dick warmly upon his masterpiece. It was evident that he meant to secure it at any cost, therefore the price was soon arranged; and before we had been there half an hour, my companion had a cheque for four figures in his pocket.

We were about to make our adieux, but the Count would not hear of it.

"Dinner will be ready almost immediately," he said. "You must stay. We are quite *en famille*, you know. Only my wife and I."

A few moments later the door opened, and there was the rustle of a silken train.

"Ah, here's the Countess!" exclaimed the millionaire, stepping forward to introduce us.

We turned, and saw a pale, beautiful woman, attired in a handsome dinner-gown.

"Ethel! You?" we both cried in amazement.

"Dick!" she gasped. "You—you have found me!"

She reeled backwards, and before we could save her, fell senseless to the floor.

A few words of excuse and explanation, and we left the Count, who, kneeling beside his wife and endeavouring to resuscitate her, was completely mystified at the strange recognition. Dick, almost beside himself with grief at discovering his idol already married, returned at once to London, while I remained at an inn at Oxted in order to glean some further information.

Inquiries showed that the Count had met her while travelling in America, and had married her. Since that time they had apparently lived happily, and not a breath of scandal had besmirched her fair name. The reason she always refused us her address was now clear; and it was evident that, while in residence at her London house in Park Lane, she had been in the habit of paying us visits unknown to her husband, assuming the character of an unmarried and flighty *Bohemienne*.

On the following day I called at the Park to inquire after the Countess's health.

The footman looked pale and grave when I asked after her ladyship.

"I much regret to inform you, sir, that my mistress is dead," he said.

"Dead?" I cried. "Impossible!"

"Yes, sir. Her maid discovered her in her boudoir late last night, and found that she had taken an overdose of morphia. We sent for the doctor, but before his arrival life was extinct. The Count is insane with grief, more especially because the maid discovered that her ladyship had left a letter to some man she calls Dick, telling him that she loved him, and could live no longer."

DICK RARELY SMILES, AND IS invariably gloomy and sad, poor fellow. The Count, ignorant of the truth, has hung his latest purchase in the private gallery of his great palace in Rome, little dreaming that the "Masked Circe" is actually the picture of his dead wife.

IV

The Man with the Fatal Finger

Three years ago, while I was writing a novel which deals with Nihilism, and which brought the heavy hand of the Press Bureau at Petersburg upon me, I contrived, in order to sketch my characters from life, to obtain an introduction to the little colony of Russian revolutionists which exists in secret in a northwestern suburb of London. I eventually won their confidence, and ingratiated myself with them by advocating Russian freedom in a series of articles in a certain London journal, which had the effect of enlisting public sympathy with the exiles in such a manner, that the editor received a number of donations, which he handed to me, while I in turn conveyed the money to my friend, Paul Grigorovitch, the head of the branch of the Narodnoe Pravo.

I was sitting at home, reading and smoking, in a very lazy mood, one winter's evening, when the servant girl entered and handed me a soiled, crumpled letter, which, she said, had been left by a strange-looking foreign woman. This did not surprise me, for I sometimes received mysterious unsigned notes from my friends the refugees when they desired to see me. The exiles are continually under the observation of the "Okhrannoe Otdelenie," or Secret Police attached to the Russian Embassy, hence the cautiousness of their movements.

I tore the envelope open and read its contents.

The words, written in a fine educated hand,—evidently a woman's,—were: "Come to Springfield Lodge, St. Margaret's Road, Regent's Park, to-night at nine. Important."

I confess the communication puzzled me, for I knew no one living at the address, and the handwriting was unfamiliar. Nevertheless, I resolved to obey the summons.

With some little difficulty I found the house. It stood back from the road, concealed behind a high wall. The thoroughfare was very quiet and eminently respectable. Each house stood in its own grounds, and had an air of wealth and prosperity about it, while the bare black branches of the great trees on either side of the road met overhead, forming a long avenue.

I gave the summons used at Grigorovitch's, namely, four distinct tugs at the bell; and presently the heavy door was opened by a Russian maid-servant.

"Who are you?" she demanded in broken English.

I told her my name, and showed her the note I had received.

"*Harosho*! Step this way, sir, if you please," she exclaimed, when she had examined the letter by the feeble light shed by a neighbouring street lamp. Then she closed the door and walked before me through a well-kept garden up to the house. Entering, she conducted me to a small and rather well-furnished apartment, the French windows of which opened out upon a spacious tennis-lawn. Around the walls were hung several choice paintings, and I noticed that upon the table lay a number of pamphlets similar to those which the organisation were secretly circulating throughout the Empire of the Tzar.

In a few moments the door opened, and a very pretty young Russian lady of about twenty-three years of age came forward to meet me.

"Good-evening," she said, smiling. "My father will be here in a few minutes. You will not object to wait, will you?"

I assured her I was in no hurry, whereupon she begged me to be seated, at the same time producing a large box of cigarettes, offering me one, and, in accordance with Russian etiquette, taking one herself.

She struck a vesta and lit hers quite naturally. Then, as she seated herself upon a low chair, I recognised that she was very handsome, and that every lineament and feature was perfect. Her countenance had an expression of charming ingenuousness and blushing candour, while her dark brilliant eyes had an intense and bewitching glance. In her brown hair was a handsome crescent of diamonds, and her evening dress of soft black net disclosed her white chest and arms.

"Were you surprised at my curt note?" she asked suddenly, blowing a cloud of smoke from her pursed-up lips.

"Well, to tell the truth, I was," I admitted. "You see, we are strangers."

"Ah, I forgot! I suppose I ought to introduce myself," she said, laughing. "I'm Prascovie Souvaroff. I know your name, and have heard how you assisted our cause."

After I had acknowledged the compliment, we commenced a commonplace conversation, which was interrupted by the entrance of a tall, elderly man, whose thin face, sunken cheeks, and deeply furrowed brow were indicative of heavy toil or long imprisonment.

Prascovie rose quickly and introduced him.

"Ivan Souvaroff, my father," she exclaimed, and when we had exchanged greetings, she said, "Now I'll go, because you want to talk. When you have finished your conversation, ring the bell, and I will return and bore you." And, laughing gaily, she tripped out of the room.

Souvaroff took a cigarette, lit it, and, seating himself thoughtfully, looked into my face and said—

"I have to thank you for coming here to-night, sir; but the matter about which I desired to see you is one of urgency. I have heard from Grigorovitch and others how you have assisted us in London and in Petersburg, and I thought it probable you would render me a small personal service."

"If it is in my power, I shall be most happy," I replied.

"It is quite easy if you will only do it; it is merely to insert a paragraph in the papers as news. I have it here, ready written." Then, taking a slip of paper from his pocket, he read the following announcement: "Prascovie, only daughter of Ivan Souvaroff, who escaped from Siberia after five years at the mines, died in London yesterday."

"Died?" I repeated, in surprise. "What do you mean? Your daughter was here, alive and well, a few moments ago!"

"I'm aware of that," he replied, smiling mysteriously. "You are not one of Us, otherwise I could tell you the reason."

"Does she know?"

"No, no," he exclaimed quickly. "Don't tell her. Promise to keep the matter strictly secret. If you publish the paragraph, I will see she does not get hold of a copy of the paper."

"Very well," I said; "I'll do as you wish."

It was a puzzling paragraph, but I had already ceased to be astonished at any action on the part of these men, for the more I thought over their secrets, the more complicated they always appeared.

As he handed me the piece of paper, with an expression of earnest thanks, I noticed that he wore a glove upon his right hand, and commented mentally that it was a rather unusual custom to wear one glove while in the house.

A few moments after he had rung the bell, Prascovie returned, followed by the servant, bearing a steaming *samovar*.

"You've not been very long over your business," she remarked, glancing at me with a smile. "Now it's all over, let's talk."

I was nothing loth to do this, and she and I resumed our chat. Then Souvaroff related the story of his imprisonment, his transportation to

Siberia, his work in the Kara silver mines, and his subsequent escape and journey to England, where he had been joined by his daughter. Some English people thought, said he, that Russia was not prepared for the freedom the Narodnoe Pravo would like to see it possess; but he assured me that the time for autocracy was past, that the Tzar's Empire had outgrown the period of benevolent despotism, and that the Russian people were quite capable of governing themselves. When he had described some of the exciting adventures connected with his escape, Prascovie, who had handed me some tea and lemon, seated herself at the piano and sang an old Russian love-song in a sweet contralto, full of harmony and tenderness.

In the meantime, her father had left us, and when she had finished, she turned upon the music-stool, and with few forewords inquired the nature of Souvaroff's business with me. Of course, I was compelled to refuse to satisfy her curiosity, and at my request she returned to the instrument and commenced another song. As she sang the second verse, there mingled with the music sounds of loud talking, boisterous laughter, and greetings in Russian, which proceeded from the hall. Evidently some one had arrived, and was being welcomed by my host.

Prascovie heard it, and ceased playing.

For a moment she sat in an attentive attitude. I noticed her face wore an expression of intense anxiety and that the colour had fled from her cheeks.

A few moments later I distinguished the voice of the servant answering her master, and after some further conversation a man exclaimed—

"*Dobroi notsche*, Souvaroff." ("Good-night.")

To this the man addressed replied in a cheery tone, the front door slammed, and my host returned into the room.

As he entered, he uttered some words in Polish *patois* to his daughter. It must have been some announcement of a startling character, for, uttering an ejaculation of alarm, she reeled and almost fell.

In a moment, however, she had recovered herself, and sank into an armchair in a grave, dejected attitude. All the light had left her face, and with her chin resting upon her breast she gazed down in thoughtful silence upon the rosettes on her little morocco slippers.

Souvaroff appeared to have aged ten years since he left the room half an hour before, and although I endeavoured to resume our conversation, he only replied in monosyllables.

I marvelled at this sudden change. Even if an unwelcome visitor had called, I could see no reason why such a strange effect should be produced.

I remained to supper, after which Prascovie threw a shawl about her shoulders and walked with me to the gate. I expressed a desire to call again and spend another evening in listening to the passionate Caucausian songs, but she appeared strangely indifferent. She merely wished me "*Prostchai*" very formally, and when we shook hands, she drew back, and I fancied she shuddered.

Then I turned away, and the gate was locked behind me.

Slowly I walked along the deserted road, absorbed in thought. The night was bright and frosty, and there was no sound save the echo of my own footsteps. I had been strolling along for perhaps five minutes, when suddenly I saw some object lying across the pavement. The thoroughfare was very inadequately lit; indeed, so dark was it that I was unable to distinguish the nature of the obstacle.

Bending down, I passed my hands rapidly over it. I found it was a man.

He was evidently drunk, therefore I resorted to the expedient of giving him a gentle but firm kick in the ribs, at the same time urging him to wake up. This, however, had no effect; therefore, after repeated efforts to rouse him, I struck a vesta and held it close to his head.

The moment I saw the yellow pallor of the face and look of unutterable horror in the glazing eyes, I knew the truth. He was dead!

His age was not more than thirty-five. He had grey eyes, fair hair and beard, and from his dress I judged that he belonged to the upper class. The heavy overcoat he wore was unbuttoned, and a silk muffler was wrapped lightly around his throat.

A glance sufficed to ascertain that he was beyond human aid, and after a moment's hesitation, I started off in search of a constable.

I was not long in finding one, and we returned to where the body lay. Other assistance was quickly forthcoming, and, a doctor residing in the neighbourhood having made an examination and pronounced life extinct, the remains were conveyed to the mortuary. Owing to the lateness of the hour and the quietness of the neighbourhood, there was no crowd of curious onlookers, nor was there anything to create horror, for no marks of violence could be discovered on the body.

At the inquest duly held I attended and gave evidence. The medical testimony went to show that the unknown man had died suddenly owing to an affection of the heart, and the jury returned a verdict of "death from natural causes." Nothing was discovered in the pockets which could lead to the unfortunate man's identification, and although his description was circulated by the police, the body was buried three days later in a nameless grave.

I had published the strange obituary notice Souvaroff had given me, and on the day of the inquest I again called at Springfield Lodge. Only Prascovie and the servant were at home. I had a pleasant *tete-a-tete* with the fair Russian, and as we sat together, I commenced to relate my discovery on the night of my previous visit.

"Ah," she exclaimed, interrupting me, "you need not tell me! I—I saw from the newspapers that you had found him. The inquest was held to-day. I'm so anxious to know the verdict."

I told her, and an exclamation of relief involuntarily escaped her. This did not strike me as peculiar at the time, but I recollected the incident afterwards, and was much puzzled at its significance.

"Do they know his name?" she asked eagerly.

"No. There was nothing to serve as a clue to his identity."

"Poor fellow!" she sighed sympathetically. "I wonder who he was."

Then our conversation turned upon other topics. We smoked several cigarettes, and, after remaining an hour, I bade her adieu and departed, half bewitched by her grace and beauty.

When, however, I called a week later and gave the usual four tugs at the bell, my summons remained unanswered. A dozen times I repeated it, but with the same effect, until a postman who chanced to pass informed me that the occupants had gone away suddenly five days before and left no address.

Surprised at this hurried departure, I walked to the house of Grigorovitch, about half a mile distant, and told him of my friends and their flight.

"Well," he said, with a smile, when I had told him their name, and explained the various circumstances, "I shrewdly suspect you've been tricked. I know no one by the name of Souvaroff. He is certainly not one of Us, and it is equally certain that he got you to insert that extraordinary paragraph by a very neat ruse."

And he laughed heartily, enjoying a joke that I confess I was unable to appreciate.

Eight months passed, during which the strange incident gradually faded from my mind.

The increased number of persons who were being sent from all parts of Russia to Siberia without trial had become a subject of much comment in England. Horrifying reports anent the state of the *etapes*, and the shocking brutality and inhuman treatment to which the oft-times innocent convicts were subjected, were continually reaching London from various sources, and public feeling against Russian autocracy had risen to fever heat.

Hence it was that one day when I entered my office I received instructions to proceed without delay to Siberia, in order to inspect the general condition of the prisoners and ascertain the truth of the harrowing details. The prospect of this mission delighted me, for not only was it certain to be fraught with a good deal of exciting adventure, but it would also enable me to complete the novel, already half written, and which I had been compelled to put aside owing to lack of information regarding life in the Asiatic penal settlements.

That evening, after calling upon Grigorovitch and informing him of my projected journey, I returned home, and sat at my writing-table far into the night, finishing some work upon which I had been engaged. The whole of the following day I spent in packing my traps, and otherwise preparing for a long absence. In the evening, while I was busy writing some letters, the servant announced that a young lady, who refused her name, desired to see me. I was not particularly clean, and I confess that just then I was too much engaged in making arrangements for my departure to think of anything else. However, my curiosity got the better of me, and I told her to admit the stranger.

"You?" I cried, when a moment later Prascovie Souvaroff entered.

"Yes. Why not?" she asked, laughing, and offering me her hand.

What could I say? I stammered out a greeting, invited her to be seated, and began to question her regarding her sudden disappearance.

To my questions she replied—

"It was imperative. You English know nothing of the persecution which follows those who flee from the wrath of the White Tzar. We were compelled to leave hurriedly, and as the Secret Police were watching both you and me it was unsafe for us to meet. To-night I have risked coming to you for a most important purpose," she added, looking up into my face earnestly.

"Oh! What's that?" I asked.

"I want you to take me to Siberia."

"To Siberia? You?" I repeated in astonishment.

"Yes. I hear you are going. Any news affecting us travels rapidly. I—I have an intense desire to see what the country beyond the Urals is like."

"Who told you I was going?"

"I'm not at liberty to say," she replied. "All I ask is that I may be allowed to accompany you. I have here sufficient money to defray the cost of my journey;" and she drew from the breast of her dress a large packet of Russian bank-notes.

I shook my head, replying that Siberia was no place for a delicately-reared woman, and pointed out the uninviting prospect of a winter journey of five thousand miles in a sleigh. "Besides," I added, "your connection with the Terrorists would render it unsafe for you to return to Russia; and, again, there are *les convenances* to be studied."

"Do you think that I, a Russian, am afraid of a cold sleigh journey?" she asked earnestly, after a few moments' silence. "Scarcely! Of course, I should not travel in this dress, but would assume the disguise of a Russian lad, in order to act as your servant and interpreter. As for *les convenances*"—and, shrugging her shoulders, she pulled a little grimace, and added, "Bah! we are not lovers!"

I asked for news of her father, but she informed me that he was in Zurich. She refused to give me her address, and all argument was useless. The point she urged, that she would be companion and interpreter combined, impressed me, and ere I had finally promised, she had given me instructions that I should, in applying for my passport from the Russian Embassy, also make application for one for "Ivan Ivanovitch, servant."

Four evenings later, I was on the platform at Charing Cross Station, watching my big iron-bound trunks being stowed away into the Continental express, and chatting to two old Fleet Street friends, who had come to see the last of me, when a rather short young man, enveloped in a long, heavy ulster, approached, and, touching his cap respectfully, said—

"Good-evening, sir. I hope I'm not late."

"No, plenty of time," I said indifferently, although I had a difficult task to keep my countenance. Turning to my friends, I explained, "That's my interpreter, Ivanovitch." Meanwhile, the object of our attention had walked across to the van to see his own trunk placed with mine.

Five minutes afterwards, when we were in the carriage together, gliding out over the bridge that spans the Thames, I burst into a hearty laugh as I, for the first time, regarded her critically. Her disguise was so complete that, for the moment when she had greeted me, I had been deceived. Laughing at her successful make-up, she removed her round fur cap, and showed how she had contrived, by cutting her hair shorter, to make it appear like a man's. Underneath her overcoat she wore a suit of thick, rough tweed, and with great gusto she related how she had filled up her large boots with wool.

She produced the inevitable cigarettes, and we spent the two hours between London and Queenborough in smoking and chatting.

To describe in detail our long railway journey across Europe by way of Berlin and Moscow would occupy too much space. Suffice it to say that I travelled through Holy Russia with a passport which bore the *vise* of the Minister of the Interior at Petersburg, and which ensured myself and my "servant" civility and attention on the part of police officials.

At length we passed through the Urals and alighted at Ekaterinbourg, where the railway at that time ended. A fortnight after leaving London, I purchased a sleigh, hired three Government horses, and Prascovie and I, in the great fur coats, skin gloves, and sheepskin boots we had bought, took our seats; the baggage and provisions having been packed in the bottom of the conveyance, and covered with a layer of straw. Then our driver shouted to the little knot of persons who had assembled before the post-station, whipped up the three shaggy horses, and away we started on the first stage of our long, dreary drive across Siberia. Over the snow the horses galloped noiselessly, and the bells on the wooden arch over their heads tinkled merrily as we moved swiftly along through the sharp, frosty air.

Soon we were out upon the Great Post Road, and as far as the eye could see, there was no other object visible on the broad, snow-covered plain but the long straight line of black telegraph poles and striped verst-posts that marked our route.

Day after day we continued our journey, often passing through miles of gloomy pine forests, and then out again upon the great barren steppes. Frequently we met convoys of convicts, pitiful, despairing bands of men and women, dragging their clanking chains with them wearily, and trudging onward towards a life to which death would be preferable. No mercy was shown them by their mounted escorts, for if a prisoner stumbled and fell from sheer exhaustion, he was beaten back to his senses with the terrible knout which each Cossack carried.

On dark nights we halted at post-houses, but when the moon shone, we continued our drive, snatching sleep as best we could. We lived upon our tinned meats and biscuits, the post-houses—which are usually about twenty to thirty miles apart—supplying tea and other necessaries.

Although the journey was terribly monotonous and uncomfortable, with a biting wind, and the intense white of the snow affecting one's eyes painfully, my fair fellow-traveller uttered no word of complaint. All day she would sit beside me chatting in English, laughing, smoking cigarettes, and now and then carrying on a conversation in Russian with our black-bearded, fierce-looking driver, afterwards interpreting his observations. Indeed, it appeared that the further we travelled from civilisation, the more light-hearted she became.

Arriving at last at Tomsk, we remained there three weeks, during which time I visited the *kameras* of the "forwarding prison," the horrors of which I afterwards fully described. An open letter I had from the Minister of the Interior admitted me everywhere, but I was compelled to secrete the notes I made in the money-belt I wore under my clothes, otherwise they would have been discovered and confiscated by the prying *ispravniks*, or police officers, during the repeated examination of our baggage at almost every small town we passed through.

Since leaving England, time had slipped rapidly away, until, one day, after we had left Tomsk, and were well on our way towards Yeniseisk, I chanced to take out my diary. I discovered that it was the last day of the old year.

The journey had been most cheerless and wearisome. It was now about four o'clock in the afternoon, and the sun, which had struggled out for half an hour, had sunk upon the hazy horizon, leaving a pale yellow streak in the grey lowering sky. An icy wind blew in fierce gusts across the barren steppe; the monotony of the dull thud of the horses' hoofs in the snow and the incessant jingle of the bells had grown utterly unendurable. The only stoppage we had made that day was about noon, when we changed horses, and Prascovie had then told me she felt very fatigued. Almost hidden under her furs, she was now sleeping soundly. Her head had fallen upon my shoulder; and I—well, although I tried to console myself with a cigar, I confess I was thinking of the folk at home, and had the nostalgia of England upon me. Suddenly she moved uneasily, and awoke with a start. She addressed a question to the driver, which he answered.

"You must be terribly tired," I said, recollecting that it was two days since we drove out of Tomsk, and that, owing to the lack of accommodation at the post-houses, we had been unable to rest.

"No, I'm not very tired," she replied. "But I feel so cramped and cold."

"Never mind," I said cheerfully, placing my arm tenderly around her waist and drawing her closer to me: "in a couple of hours we shall get something hot to eat." She did not answer, but in a few moments she again fell asleep with her head upon my shoulder; and I, too, also dozed off.

Our lonely halting-place was, like all Siberian post-houses, built of pine logs, and little better than a large hut, devoid of any vestige of comfort, and horribly dirty. The sitting-room was a bare, uncarpeted place, with a large brick stove in the centre, a picture of the Virgin upon the wall, a wooden table, and three or four rough chairs, while the little dens that served as sleeping apartments contained nothing beyond a chair and a straw mattress.

It was not long after our arrival that the great *samovar* was placed upon the table, and, together with the two sinister-looking fellows who kept the place, we sat down to a rough, uncivilised meal. The evening we spent in smoking and drinking vodka, Prascovie and I being able to carry on a private conversation by speaking English.

I asked why she was so unusually thoughtful, but she replied that it was only because she was in need of rest.

"I am sorry I am breaking down," she said apologetically, and laughing at the same time. "But I'm only a woman. It was, indeed, very kind of you to have been bothered with me."

"Don't mention it," I said. "I'm sure I'm indebted to you, for your knowledge of Russian assists me in my work. Do you remember," I added, "that it is a year to-night since we first met?"

"Was it?" she asked in a strange tone of alarm. "Ah, I remember. I—I was happy then, wasn't I?"

"Are you not happy now?" I inquired.

"Yes—very," she replied, smiling. "But I'm tired, and must go to my room, or I shall be fit for nothing to-morrow."

"Very well," I replied. "I'll tell you to go in a few minutes."

Then, after joining the driver and post-house keepers in another glass of vodka, I said to her—

"Ivan, you can go. I shall require you no longer."

Gathering up her coat, hat and gloves, she bowed, and, wishing the men "Good-night," went to her room.

After smoking for another hour, I also sought my dirty little den. In the heart of Siberia one must expect to rough it, therefore I took my revolver from my belt, placed it under my pillow, and, after removing some of my clothes, strapped my fur rug around my neck, and, stretching myself upon the hard pallet, soon dropped off to sleep.

Next morning, when I had dressed, I knocked several times at Prascovie's door, but received no reply. Subsequently I pushed it open and entered, discovering, to my surprise, that the room was empty.

Notwithstanding my limited knowledge of Russian, I managed to make the men understand that my servant was missing, and they searched the premises, but without avail. They examined the road outside, but, as it had been snowing heavily during the night, no footprints were visible.

Prascovie had mysteriously disappeared!

While I remained in charge of the post-house, the three men mounted the horses and rode out in different directions, thinking it possible that she had strayed away upon the steppe and become lost in a snowdrift. Towards evening, however, they returned, after a long and futile search.

Anxious to solve the mystery, and reluctant to leave without her, I remained there several days. As the nearest dwelling was twenty miles distant, and her overcoat and hat still remained in her room, her disappearance was all the more puzzling. I examined her box, but found nothing in it except articles of male wearing apparel; so after a week of anxious waiting, I became convinced that to remain there longer was useless.

With heavy heart, and sorely puzzled over the mystery, I continued my lonely journey towards the mines of Yeniseisk. Having inspected them, I journeyed south, alone and dejected, and investigated the great prisons at Krasnoiarsk and Irkutsk, afterwards returning through Omsk and Tobolsk, and thence to the Urals and civilisation.

I missed her companionship very much, and long before my journey ended, I had grown dull, morose, and melancholy.

After an absence of six months, I again returned to London. When I arrived home, fatigued and hungry, and before I had time to cast off my worn-out travelling suit, the servant girl handed me a small packet which she said had arrived by registered post a week before.

It had a Russian stamp upon it, and bore the postmark of Kiakhta, a small town south of Irkutsk, on the border of Mongolia.

Breaking open the seals, I found a small box, from which I took a thick gold ring, set with a magnificent diamond.

Attached to it was a small piece of paper which bore, in a man's handwriting, the following words:—

"The husband of Prascovie Souvaroff, who owes to you the safe return of his beloved wife, sends this little gift as a slight recognition of the kindness she received at your hands."

There was neither, name, address, nor date; nothing to show who was the anonymous husband.

THE MYSTERY WAS SOLVED IN a most unexpected manner.

Some months after the results of my investigations had been published, I chanced one night to attend the banquet of the Association of Foreign Consuls held in the Whitehall Rooms of the Hotel Metropole. As usual, a number of the *corps diplomatique* were present, and among them Serge Velitchko, one of the *attaches* of the Russian Embassy, an old friend of mine, whom I had not seen since my return.

"I congratulate you on your lucky escape, old fellow," he exclaimed, after we had exchanged cordial greetings.

"Escape? What do you mean?" I inquired.

"Ah, it's all very well," he replied, laughing, as we strolled together into an ante-room that was unoccupied. "Prascovie was very fascinating, wasn't she?"

"How did you know?" I asked in amazement, for I imagined no one was aware that she had been my companion.

"Oh, we knew all about it, never fear," he said, with a smile. "By Jove! it was quite a romance, travelling all that distance with a pretty companion, and then losing her on the Yeniseisk Steppe. It was lucky for you, however, that she left you in time, otherwise you would, in all probability, have been working underground at Kara, or some other place equally delightful, by this time."

"Explain yourself," I urged impatiently. "You're talking in enigmas."

"Listen, and I'll let you into the secret," said my friend, casting himself lazily into a chair. "The man you knew as Souvaroff was, until about six years ago, wealthy and popular at our Court at Petersburg; but he was suspected of political intrigue, and sentenced to lifelong exile and hard labour in Siberia. After his banishment, Prascovie, who was then living at Moscow, was detected by the police distributing some revolutionary pamphlets, for which she also was sent to Siberia.

At the prison at Irkutsk father and daughter met. While there, Prince Pavlovitch Kostomaroff, the governor of the Yeniseisk province, who had previously known and admired *la belle* Souvaroff in Petersburg society, discovered her, and offered her marriage. This she accepted, and they were married privately, because, had it become known that the Prince had wedded a political exile, he would have fallen into disfavour with the Tzar. The Prince not being governor of the province in which his wife was imprisoned, a difficulty presented itself how he should obtain her release. Even Ivan Kobita, controller of the prison, was ignorant of the secret union, but it so happened that he also became enamoured of his fair captive. At length, in return for her promise to marry him, he allowed her and her father comparative freedom. As might be expected, they were not long in taking advantage of this, for within a fortnight, aided by the Prince, and provided with a passport obtained by him, they managed to escape and come to England."

"And what of Kobita?"

"He quickly discovered the ruse, and ascertained that the Prince had connived at their escape. Our Secret Police tracked the fugitives to their hiding-place in London. Still unaware that she was the Prince's wife, Kobita obtained leave of absence and came to England. Before his arrival, however, he wrote, urging her to marry him, declaring that if she refused, he would expose the Prince as aiding and abetting dangerous Nihilists. Prascovie, who clearly saw that if the truth reached the Tzar, her husband would be disgraced and deprived of liberty, was at her wits' ends. She was in desperation when, two years ago, Kobita arrived in London—"

"Was that on the night I called upon them?"

"Yes. It was on receipt of the letter from Kobita that Souvaroff sent for you and requested you to put the obituary notice in the papers, in order that when the Siberian official came to claim his daughter's hand, he could convince him of her death. But this plan was not carried out quickly enough. Kobita arrived on the night of your visit, and was received by Prascovie's father, who stated that she had gone to call upon a friend in the vicinity, and offered to send his servant to direct him to the house in question. To this Prascovie's admirer had no objection, and, shaking Souvaroff warmly by the hand, wished him *au revoir*, and started off, accompanied by the servant, in search of the imaginary neighbour. The hand-shaking proved fatal, for he had not walked far before he fell dead. The whole thing had been carefully planned, and the trusty servant, who had been instructed how to act, extracted everything from the dead man's pockets that would lead to identification. Hence his burial in a nameless grave."

"Do you assert that he was murdered?"

"Yes. We were in possession of all these facts, but refrained from causing Souvaroff's arrest, because it was not a wise policy to expose to the London public that Russia had established a bureau of secret police in their midst. Prascovie and her father hid for some months, and we lost sight of them until she called upon you, and accompanied you in disguise to Siberia. Once or twice you very narrowly escaped being apprehended; indeed, on one occasion orders were telegraphed to Tomsk for the arrest of your companion and yourself, because the declaration on your passport regarding 'Ivan Ivanovitch' was known to be false. By the intervention of a high official, however, the order was countermanded, and you were allowed to pass."

"What has become of Prascovie's father?" I asked in astonishment. "Surely he was not Kobita's murderer, for the man died of heart disease."

"You are mistaken. He died of Obeah poison. Souvaroff, who was once a consul in Hayti, knew of the secret poison which the natives extract from the gecko lizard, and which cannot be detected. So deadly is it, that one drop is sufficient to produce a fatal result, and the manner in which he administered it was somewhat novel. He prepared to receive his enemy by allowing the nail of the forefinger of his right hand to grow long, afterwards thinning it to a point as fine as a needle. Upon this point he placed the poison, and kept a glove on until Kobita's arrival. Then, in wishing him adieu, he pricked the skin of his victim while shaking hands with him, producing an effect similar to syncope."

"Where is Souvaroff now?"

"Dead. He returned to Petersburg as soon as his daughter had left with you, but was arrested and placed in solitary confinement in the Fortress. While there, he wrote a confession of the murder, and afterwards committed suicide."

"And will they arrest Prascovie?"

"No. She lives in another province to that in which she was imprisoned. No one there knows that she is an escaped convict, and as the Prince was once attached to this Embassy, we are not likely to divulge."

He chaffed me a little, laughed heartily in his good-natured way, and soon afterwards we rejoined the guests.

I have heard nothing since of my unconventional travelling companion. A short time ago, however, I received an anonymous present of furs, and I shrewdly suspect whence it came. The Prince's ring, which is the admiration and envy of many of my friends, still glitters on my finger, and I regard it as a souvenir of the most happy and romantic journey of my life.

V

SANTINA

"From the Contessa, signore."

A tall liveried servant handed me a coroneted missive, and, bowing stiffly, withdrew. Taking the letter mechanically, I sat puffing at my cigarette and dreaming.

The sultry day was over, and the full moon was shining down clear and cool. Genoa had drawn breath again; its streets and piazzas had grown alive with the stir of manifold movement; the broad Via Roma, with its fine shops and garish *cafes*, echoed with increasing confusion of voices and jest and laughter and song; while the flower-sellers were everywhere, and the newsboys in strident tones cried the *Secolo* and the *Gazzetta*. My small and rather shabby room was on the top floor of a great old palazzo in the Via Balbi. The jalousies, wide-open, admitted little gusts of fresh air that blew up from the sea, while the ceaseless babel of tongues, the clip-clap of horses' hoofs, and the indescribable odour of garlic, fried oil, and the cheap cigars characteristic of an Italian street, was borne in upon me.

Two candles in the sconces of a small Venetian mirror shed their light over the pedestal, upon which was a statue almost finished. It was a representation of a lovely woman in carnival dress, that I had chiselled in marble.

The face was absolutely beautiful, not only because of its perfect harmony, not only winsome in the gentleness of its contour, but it was also masterful by virtue of the freedom and force expressed in all its firmness.

Lazily I opened the letter, and prepared to feast upon its contents. But the few brief words penned in a woman's hand caused me to start to my feet in anger and dismay; and, holding my breath, I crushed the missive and cast it under my foot. She who had written to me was the original of this statue, which was considered my masterpiece.

The note was cold and formal, unlike her usual graceful letters. It stated that she was leaving Italy that evening; and expressed regret she could not sit again to me. She also enclosed a bank-note for two thousand lire, which she apparently believed would repay me for my trouble.

My trouble! *Dio mio*! Had it not been a labour of love, when I adored—nay, worshipped her; and she, in her turn, had bestowed smiles and kisses upon me?

Yet she had written and sent me money, as if I were a mere tradesman; and from the tone of her note, it seemed as if our friendship existed no longer. Every day she had come to my studio, bringing with her that breath of stephanotis that always pervaded her; and because she was not averse to a mild flirtation, I had believed she loved me! Bah! I had been fooled! The iron of a wasted love, of a useless sacrifice, was in my heart.

This sudden awakening had crushed me; and I stood gazing aimlessly out of the window, unaware of the presence of a visitor, until I felt a hearty slap on the shoulder, and, turning quickly, faced my old friend, Pietro Barolini.

"*Chi vide mai tanto!*" he cried cheerily. "Why, my dear fellow, you look as if you've got a very bad attack of melancholia. What's the matter?"

"Read that," I said, pointing to the crumpled letter on the floor. "Tell me, what am I to do?"

Picking up the note, he read it through, drew a heavy breath, and remained silent and thoughtful.

Pietro and I had been companions ever since our childhood days, when, as bare-legged urchins, sons of honest fishermen, we had played on the beach at our quiet home in rural Tuscany. When we set out together to seek our fortunes, Fate directed us to Genoa; and in "La Superba" we still lived, Pietro having become a well-known musician; while I, Gasparo Corazzini, had, by a vagary of chance, attracted the notice of the great *maestro* Verga, under whose tuition I had developed into a successful sculptor.

"It is unfortunate," my friend said at last, twisting his pointed black moustache; "yet she is not of our world, and, after all, perhaps it is best that you should part."

"Ah!" I said. "Your words are well meant, Pietro; but I love her too passionately to cast aside her memory so lightly. I must see her. She must tell me from her own lips that she no longer cares for me!" I cried, starting up impetuously.

"Very well—go. Take her back the money with which she has insulted you, and bid adieu to her forever. You will soon forget."

"Yes," I said; "I will."

Snatching up my hat, and crushing the letter into the pocket of my blouse, I rushed out and down the stairs into the street, without a thought of personal appearance, my only desire being to catch her before she departed.

Blindly I hurried across the Piazza del Principe, then out of the town into the open country, never slackening my pace for a moment until I entered the grounds of a great white villa that stood on the hillside at Comigliano, overlooking the moonlit sea. Then, with a firm determination to be calm, I advanced towards the house cautiously, and, swinging myself upon the low verandah, peered in at a glass door that stood open.

Noiselessly I entered. The room was dazzling in its magnificence, notwithstanding that the lamps were shaded by soft lace and tinted silk. The gilt furniture, the great mirrors, the statuary—genuine works by Leopardi and Sansovino—the Persian rugs and rich silken hangings, all betokened wealth, taste, and refinement.

Reclining on a couch with languid grace, clad in a loose wrapper of dove-grey silk, with her hair *en deshabille*, was the woman I loved.

"Santina!" I whispered, bending over her, uttering a pet name I had bestowed upon her.

She started, and jumped up quickly, half-frightened, exclaiming—

"*Cielo*! You, Gasparo—you *here*?"

"Yes," I replied, catching her white bejewelled hand and kissing it. "Yes. Why not?"

She snatched away her hand quickly, and passed it wearily across her brow. Her beauty shone with marvellous radiance, for she was only twenty-four—fair-haired, blue-eyed, and with a slim, graceful figure that gave her an almost girlish appearance. I own myself entranced by her loveliness.

"I thought," she said, after a moment's hesitation—"I thought my note explained everything. The statue is practically finished, and—"

"No—no!" I cried. "It is still incomplete. You cannot—you shall not leave me, Santina!"

"Pray, why?" she asked indignantly, raising her eyebrows.

"Because—because I love you," I stammered.

"Love!" she exclaimed, with a light laugh. "Bah! How foolish! Love! It is only plebeians and fools who love. There is no such word in our vocabulary."

"Yes, yes," I said quickly. "I know the insurmountable barrier that lies between us, Santina. But do you intend to leave Italy—to leave me alone—now?"

"Of course. It is not my intention to return for several years; perhaps never. We have spent many pleasant hours together; but you have become infatuated, therefore we must part."

"No!" I cried; "I cannot—I will not let you go! Only a week ago you confessed that you loved me. What have I done that you should treat me so?"

She made no immediate answer; and as she stood with bowed head and somewhat pale, thoughtful face, I wondered what mystery veiled and troubled her clear, resolute nature.

Placing my arm around her waist, I bent and kissed her lips; but she struggled to free herself.

"*Dio!*" she cried hoarsely. "Why have you come here, Gasparo? Think of my reputation—my honour! If any one found you here alone with me, and I in *deshabille.*"

"Tell me, Santina, do you still love me?" I asked earnestly, looking into her eyes.

"I—I hardly know," she replied, with a strange, preoccupied air.

"Why are you leaving so suddenly?"

"Because it is imperative," she replied. "But hush! listen! a voice! *Dio! it is my husband!*"

"Your husband!" I gasped. "What do you mean? I thought the Count died in Buenos Ayres two years ago, and that you were free?"

"So did I. But that was his voice. *Cielo!* I know it, alas! too well," she said, turning deathly pale.

Rushing suddenly across the room, she snatched something from a small niche in the wall and brought it over to me. It was a curious little ivory idol, about six inches long, representing Amida, the eternal Buddha. Kissing it, she handed it to me, saying—

"Quick! take this as a souvenir. It has been my talisman; may it be yours. When I am absent, look upon it sometimes, Gasparo, and think of me."

"You do love me, then, Santina?" I cried joyously; for answer she placed her lips to mine.

"Hide! hide at once!" she implored. "Kneel behind that screen, or we are lost. Remain there until we have left the house, and tell no one that you have seen the Count. *A rivederci!*"

I slipped into the place she indicated, and not a moment too soon, for as I did so, a short, stout man of about sixty years of age entered. His face wore a strange, fixed expression, and as he strode in, he betrayed no astonishment at meeting his wife, although she, terrified and trembling, shrank from him.

"I thought you were ready," he exclaimed roughly. "Be quick and put on your travelling dress. The carriage is on its way round, and we haven't a moment to spare if we mean to leave to-night."

"I shall not keep you long," she sighed, and a few moments later they both turned and left the room.

The reappearance of the Count di Pallanzeno, whom every one believed had died, was puzzling, and the manner in which husband and wife conversed showed there was but little affection between them.

Suddenly I remembered that I had forgotten to return the bank-note, but I saw it was useless to attempt to do so now, therefore I decided to keep it until we met again. Obeying the Contessa's instructions, I remained in my hiding-place for half an hour, until I heard the carriage drive away down the road, then I stole out upon the verandah and let myself down noiselessly into the garden.

The moon was shining brilliantly on the white blossoms and the pale marbles, and in order to escape the observation of any of the servants who might be about, I crept along under the dark shadow of the ilex-trees in the direction of the road. I had not gone very far when suddenly I caught my foot in an obstruction, and, stumbling, fell over some object that lay in my path. Regaining my feet, I bent to ascertain the cause of my fall, when, to my amazement, I discovered it was a man.

I touched the face, and drew back in horror. *The man was dead*!

Everything was quiet, not a leaf stirred, so, taking the body under the arms, I dragged it out into the light. The silver moonbeam that fell across the white face of the corpse gave it a ghastly appearance, revealing the features of a well-dressed man of middle age, totally unknown to me.

Closer examination disclosed that a murder had been committed. The man had been shot in the back.

Searching about the spot, I was not long before I discovered the weapon with which the crime had evidently been committed. It was a five-chambered plated revolver, one cartridge of which had been discharged. As I inspected it in the cold, bright light, eager to find a clue to the murderer, my eyes fell upon two words engraved on the barrel.

Breathlessly I deciphered them, and then stood dumb with awe and dismay. *The name engraved upon it was my own*!

In a moment a terrible thought flashed across me. Was not my presence there, and the discovery of a revolver bearing my name, direct circumstantial evidence against me? Thus recognising my danger, I put the weapon in my pocket, cast a final glance at the dead man's face, and, creeping noiselessly away under the high hedge of rhododendron and jessamine, I at length gained the road and returned to the noisy city.

In the Bourse, in the Galleria Mazzini, in the streets, in the *cafes*, everywhere, one topic only was discussed next day. A startling tragedy had been enacted, for, according to the newspapers, Colonel Rossano had been discovered mysteriously murdered in the gardens of the Villa Pallanzeno.

No motive for the assassination could be assigned, for the colonel, who had only arrived on the previous day from Milan, was a most popular and distinguished officer. The police, it was stated, had received instructions from the Ministry of the Interior at Rome to spare no effort to discover the assassin, and the King himself had offered a reward of ten thousand lire for any information which would lead to the arrest of the murderer.

During the hour of the siesta, I had stretched myself in an old armchair in the studio, smoking, when Pietro burst into the room, greeting me with that buoyancy habitual to him. I asked him if he had heard of the tragedy, and gave him the papers to read. Having eagerly scanned them, he expressed surprise that the shot was not heard.

"I suppose the Contessa does not know anything of it," I said. "The body was not discovered until after midnight, whereas she left by the mail for Turin at ten o'clock."

"And what was the result of your interview?" he asked, seating himself on the edge of the table, and carelessly swinging his legs.

"She has gone, but she will return," I replied briefly.

"And she still loves you—eh?"

"Yes; you guess correctly," I laughed.

"So goes the world! How happy you should be—you, the accepted lover of the girl-widow of a millionaire! One of these days you'll marry, and then *per Bacco*! you'll throw over your old companion, the humble fiddler of the Politeama."

His jesting words reminded me of the reappearance of the Count, that Santina was not free, and that our love was illicit.

"No," I said sorrowfully; "I may love, but I shall never marry her."

THREE YEARS PASSED, LONG, WEARY years, during which I had waited patiently for Santina's return. *Ahi sorte avversa!*

The villa remained in just the same condition, but none of the servants knew the whereabouts of their mistress, and it had been whispered that the police, in order to learn something of events on the night of the murder, had vainly endeavoured to trace her.

With me things went badly. True, the statue of the Countess, that I had christened "Folly," had gained a medal at the International Exhibition at Turin, but my later works had proved ignominious failures. I thought nothing of Art, only of the woman who had entranced me, and my hand had somehow lost its cunning. The carved Amida had brought me ill-fortune, it seemed, for I was now at the end of my resources.

Pietro had long ago accepted a lucrative post in the orchestra at La Scala, at Milan, and I lived alone and friendless in the old palazzo.

One evening, when Genoa was in *festa*, I had starved all day, and in desperation I at last resolved to change the bank-note Santina had sent me. Putting on my hat, I descended the stairs into the gaily-decked street, and pushed my way through the laughing crowd in the Via Nouvissima, at last turning into the narrow Via degli Orefici in search of a money-changer's. A group of children were playing under a dark, ancient archway. How happy they seemed, with their bright chubby faces, like the carved cupids and cherubs in San Lorenzo!

All the world was gay, and I alone was desolate. The little office I entered was kept by a hook-nosed Jew, who, when I asked for gold in exchange for the limp piece of paper, took it and examined it carefully through his hornrimmed spectacles. Taking a book from a shelf, he consulted it, started, and then looked sharply up at me.

"This note," he said, "does not belong to you."

"It does," I answered indignantly.

"Can you tell me whence you obtained it?"

"It is no business of yours!" I cried.

"*Corpo di Bacco*, signore! It were best for you to answer such a simple and necessary question with at least a semblance of civility."

"Why should I, when you roundly accuse me of possessing stolen property? What grounds have you for saying the note does not belong to me?"

"I did but speak the truth. This note is not rightfully yours."

"You waste my time. Give me back the note; I will change it elsewhere."

"Signore, I *dare not* return you the note."

"And why, pray?" I asked, suppressing my angry indignation.

"*Avvertite*! It was stolen."

"Stolen?" I cried.

"Yes. Stolen from the man who was murdered at the Villa Pallanzeno three years ago. There is a big reward. I must inform the police."

I was dumbfounded. The note Santina had sent me had been filched from a murdered man? Impossible!

The old Jew was hobbling round the counter, intending to give the alarm, so, seeing my danger, I snatched the note from him, and ran away through many intricate byways until I reached my studio. Cramming a number of things I valued into my pockets, I tied up a few other necessaries in a handkerchief, and then sped downstairs again and out into the open country.

IN THE EAST, THE GREAT arc of the sky, the distant mountains and the plains, were rose-coloured with the flush of dawn, for it was the hour when night and morning met and parted. My soul was mad with baffled hope, and I was mentally and physically ill.

The softening influences of the glorious morning awoke no responsive echoes in my troubled brain, for I had walked the whole night through, and now, worn out, footsore, hungry, and altogether hopeless, I was resting beside a little wayside shrine of Our Lady of Good Counsels, and in the hazy distance could see the gold cross, red roofs, and the gleaming white towers of Florence.

For many months I had been a homeless wanderer, a mere tramp, picking up a living as best as I could, but always moving from place to place over the smiling plains of Lombardy, or among the peaceful Tuscan vineyards, fearing that the police would pounce upon me and charge me with a crime of which I was innocent.

I had tramped to Milan in search of Pietro, but he had left—gone to Naples, they thought.

I think you, in English, have something like our old Tuscan saying, "*Le sciagure e le alle-grezze non vengono mai sole.*"

Ah me! There is bitter truth in it. Misfortunes always come in overwhelming numbers, and those who are not favourites of the jade might as well be in their graves.

The more I reflected upon the strange tragedy, the more puzzling was the mystery.

WILLIAM LE QUEUX

Where was Santina? If she were innocent, why should she hide herself?

For two hours I tramped on over the dusty road to the city of Dante and Michael Angelo, at last entering the Porte Romano; and then wandering down the long street and around the Palazzo Pitti, I crossed the Vecchio Bridge, and passed on towards the great Duomo, with Brunelleschi's wondrous dome.

I had taken a drink of water at the old Renaissance fountain in the Piazza del Mercato, and was strolling quietly on, gazing in wonderment at the grand old Gothic cathedral, when suddenly a heavy hand was laid upon my shoulder, and a stern voice said—

"Gasparo Corazzini, I arrest you."

Almost before I was aware of it, two gendarmes, who had accompanied a little, shabbily-dressed police agent, seized me.

"For what crime do you lay your hands upon me?" I cried indignantly.

"You are accused of the murder of Colonel Rossano in Genoa," the detective replied.

My heart sank within me. I was spellbound by the appalling charge.

The gloomy old Assize Court at Genoa was crowded; the afternoon heat was intense; the ray of sunlight slanting through the high window lit up the time-dimmed picture of Gesu, and fell upon the great gold crucifix that hung over the head of the grave-looking President. My trial had excited the greatest interest, for the police had, with extraordinary ingenuity, pieced together a truly wonderful chain of circumstantial evidence against me; and it was remarkable how ready people were to swear my life away. I stood like one in a dream, for I had at last become convinced of Santina's treachery, and, having relinquished hope, had grown callous to everything.

I had no defence, for I had admitted being at the Villa on the night in question, and in the revolver found upon me remained some of the cartridges, the bullets of which exactly corresponded with that which caused the colonel's death.

The Prosecutor had concluded, and without heeding the words the President was addressing to me, I stood with bent head and eyes fixed upon the floor. They might do their worst; they could not heap upon me greater agony than I had already suffered.

Suddenly there was a stir in court, as a servant in the Pallanzeno livery pushed his way forward and handed a large envelope to the judge.

There were two legal-looking papers inside, and the President, having read them through twice, handed them to his two colleagues with an expression of profound surprise. A witness was called, and gabbled a statement in English which I could not understand. Then the judges retired to an ante-room, and remained absent for nearly half an hour.

Presently they returned and reseated themselves. A moment later, with startling suddenness, the words fell upon my ears—

"The prisoner, Gasparo Corazzini, is free. The murderer has confessed."

Confessed? Was it Santina or her husband who had admitted their guilt? From my guards I endeavoured to ascertain the name of the assassin. But I was told that the President had decided for the present to keep it secret, and as the Contessa's servant had disappeared, I turned and left the court.

Walking through the white sunlit streets to the Via Balbi, I mounted the stairs to my studio. The dust of months was over everything, but some one had been there during my absence.

The image of the Contessa still stood where I had left it, but its hideous appearance startled me. An arm had been broken off, and the face had been disfigured, battered beyond recognition with a heavy iron mallet that lay upon the floor.

An enemy had maliciously wrecked my masterpiece.

Sinking into a chair, I covered my face with my hands in blank despair. My reputation as a sculptor had gone, my skill with the chisel had departed. My kind master, the great Verga, had died, and I, lonely, forsaken, and forgotten, had no means of livelihood left to me.

How long I sat plunged in grim, melancholy thoughts I know not. When I returned to consciousness, the bright moon was shining full into the room, and the broken statue looked pale and ghostly in the deep shadow.

I had risen, and was standing before the window with my head sunk on my breast, when suddenly I felt a warm arm slowly entwine itself about my neck. Starting with a cry of surprise, I turned, and found to my amazement that Santina stood beside me.

"Gasparo!" she whispered softly, drawing my head down and kissing my lips.

"Santina!" I exclaimed joyfully. "You have at last returned?"

"Yes," she replied. "I—I told you we should meet again, and I have kept my promise."

She was very handsomely dressed in an evening gown of pale blue, her velvet cape was edged with sable, and, unloosened, displayed around her throat a diamond necklet that shone in the bright moonbeams a narrow line of white brilliancy.

For a few moments we stood in silence, clasped in each other's arms.

Then I commenced to question her, and she told me how she had been living far away in London, adding—

"But I have come back to you, Gasparo. You still love me, do you not?"

"Love you?" I cried. "I would give half the years of my life if you were mine."

"I am yours," she said, gazing earnestly into my eyes.

"But—but your husband?" I exclaimed.

She shrugged her shoulders carelessly and laughed. Her eyes travelled round the studio, until they fell upon the mutilated statue.

"Ah!" she cried hoarsely; "your enemy's handiwork. Then that was part of the revenge!"

"What revenge? Tell me about it!"

"A—a shadow came between us, Gasparo," she sighed. "You had a rival, although you were unaware of it, and I was afraid to tell you, because I feared you would act desperately and create a scene. The man pestered me with his attentions, but I loved you, and turned a deaf ear to him. On the evening of the tragedy he came to me surreptitiously, and, with passionate declarations, begged me to accept him, but I refused, and left the room, vowing to leave Italy, never to return. I knew not what to do, for I was afraid to confess I loved you, as I saw that a *fracas* and scandal would ensue, but at length I came to the conclusion that it would be best for both of us if we parted at least for a time, therefore I wrote you that cruel letter, in order to make you think my flirtation was at an end."

"Yes; yes," I said, eagerly drinking in every word.

"The conspiracy against us both was one of extraordinary cunning and daring. Your rival was, I have since ascertained, a French spy. On the evening in question, Colonel Rossano, who was an old friend of my father's, arrived from Milan, having been entrusted with some plans of fortifications and other important and secret documents to take to the Ministry of War at Rome. The colonel intended to remain the night with us, but your rival, by some means, knew that the documents were in his possession, and resolved to secure them. Therefore he secreted himself, and when the officer entered the garden, he shot him, afterwards taking from his pockets the plans, together with a large sum in bank-notes. It was after committing this terrible deed that he sought me; and then, when I refused him, he plotted a desperate vengeance that he intended should fall upon us both. With villainous cunning he had already caused your name to be engraved on the revolver with which he took the colonel's life, and placed the weapon beside the body. Afterwards he proceeded to carry out the other portion of the foul plot that was so nearly successful."

"What was that?" I asked, amazed at her story.

"He followed my servant Guiseppe, bribed him to give him the letter I addressed to you, and, having read its contents, enclosed one of the bank-notes he had stolen from the murdered man. He intended that when the charge of assassination was made against you owing to the revolver, corroborative evidence would be furnished by the stolen note in your possession. Towards me he acted differently. You still have that little souvenir I gave you, I suppose? Strike a light, and I will show you something."

I obeyed, and lit one of the candles, afterwards taking from my pocket the quaint little carved Amida, which I had kept carefully wrapped in a piece of chamois leather.

"See! Look at this!" she said, as she screwed off the head of the idol.

And then, holding out my hand, she emptied into my palm a piece of thin paper screwed up into the size of a nut. I spread it out, and found it was a plan of the submarine mines in Genoa harbour!

"I had only a few days previously showed him this little image, and had quite innocently told him that it was hollow, and the head could be removed," she continued. "Therefore, during my absence from the room, he must have secreted the paper there for two reasons: firstly, to get rid of it for a time; and secondly, so that he could, if so desired, throw a terrible suspicion upon me as your friend and alleged accomplice."

"But how do you know all this?" I inquired.

"For some time after I left Italy I neither saw nor heard of him. When, however, I was told of the tragedy, I admit that I felt convinced that the colonel had fallen by your hand, for I knew you were desperate that night, and knew also that you frequently carried a revolver. It was the horrible suspicion of your guilt that prevented me from returning or communicating with you. Nevertheless, a year ago, while I was living in London, this man, who had followed me, recommended his hateful attentions. His actions throughout were *belle parole e cattivi fatti*. Apparently he refrained from denouncing you because he believed he would eventually prevail upon me to marry him. For six months he shadowed me, and I humoured him until at last I again lost sight of him. One night, while still in London, I received a telegram stating that he had met with an accident, that he was dying, and that he must see me. I went, and found him in a wretched, squalid garret in a gloomy quarter they call Saffron Hill. It was there, before he died, that he made, in the presence of a notary I called in, the confession which I sent to the President of the Assize Court to-day. In an English newspaper I read the grave charge made against you, and hastened here without losing a moment."

"You have not explained," I said quickly. "You have not told me the name of my unknown rival."

"He was your friend. *His name was Pietro Barolini!*"

"Pietro!" I gasped. "Why, I considered him my warmest friend. But what of your husband? Where is he?"

"Ah, I deceived you, Gasparo!" she said, laying her hand upon my arm. "I knew you would allow me to go in peace if you believed my husband still lived, therefore I practised a ruse upon you. The man from whom you hid was my father, to whose exertions the elucidation of the mystery is in a great measure due. He has returned with me to the Villa, and I will introduce you to him this evening."

"Then the Count is not living?"

"No, Gasparo," Santina whispered softly. "He died in Buenos Ayres, as you are aware, six months after our marriage. There is no barrier now between us; the grim shadow that darkened my life has passed away, and we are free—free to love each other, and to marry."

VI

The Woman with a Blemish

The weird prologue of the drama was enacted some years ago, yet time, alas! does not obliterate it from my memory.

To the hail of bullets, the whistling of shells, the fitful flash of powder, and the thunder of guns I had grown callous. During the months I had been in Servia and Bulgaria watching and describing the terrible struggle between Turkey and Russia, I had grown world-weary, careless of everything, even of life. I had been present at the relief of Kars, had witnessed the wholesale slaughter in various parts of the Ottoman Empire, and was now attached to the Russian forces bombarding Plevna.

Those who have never experienced actual warfare cannot imagine how terrible are the horrors of life at the front.

Picture for a moment a great multitude of men whose sole occupation is slaughter—some with smoke-blackened faces toiling in the earthworks, discharging their heavy field-pieces which day and night dispatch their death-dealing missiles into the shattered town yonder, while hordes of Cossacks and Russian grenadiers engage the enemy at every point; the rattle of musketry and artillery is deafening, the rain of bullets incessant, and on every side is suffering and death. And you are a war-correspondent, a spectator, a non-combatant! You have travelled across Europe to witness this frightful carnage, and paint word-pictures of it for the folk at home. At any moment a stray bullet might end your existence; nevertheless, you must not be fatigued, for after the toil of the day your work commences, and you must find a quiet corner where you can write a column of description for transmission to Fleet Street.

Such were the circumstances in which I was placed when, after a six months' absence from England, I found myself before Plevna. The brief December day was drawing to a close as I stood, revolver in hand, near one of the great guns that at regular intervals thundered forth in chorus with the others. I was in conversation with Captain Alexandrovitch, a smart young officer with whom I was on very friendly terms, and we were watching through our field-glasses the effect of our fire upon the town.

"Now my lads," the captain shouted in Russian, to the men working the gun. "Let us test our accuracy. See! one of Osman's officers has just appeared on the small redoubt yonder to encourage his men. There is a good target. See!"

Scarcely had he spoken when the men sprang back, the great gun belched forth flame, and the shell, striking the enemy's fortification, took part of it away, blowing the unfortunate Turkish officer into fragments.

Such are the fortunes of war!

"Good!" exclaimed Alexandrovitch, laughing; as, turning to me, he added, "If we continue like this, we shall silence the redoubts before to-morrow. How suicidal of Osman Pasha to imagine his handful of lean, hungry dogs capable of defence against the army of the Great White Tzar. Bah! We shall—"

The sentence was left unfinished, for a bullet whistled close to me, and a second later he threw up his hands, and, uttering a loud cry of pain, staggered and fell, severely wounded in the side.

Our ambulance and medical staff was on that day very disorganised, so, instead of conveying him to the field hospital, they carried him into my tent, close by.

Night fell, and for hours I knelt beside him, trying to alleviate his agony. The surgeon had dressed the wound, and the officer lay writhing and groaning, while by the meagre light of an evil-smelling oil-lamp I scribbled my dispatch. At last the wounded man became quieter, and presently slept; while I, jaded and worn, wrapped my blanket about me, placed my revolver under my saddle, and lay down to snatch an hour's repose.

How long I slept I scarcely know; but I was awakened by a strange rustling.

The flap of the tent was open, and I saw against the faint grey glimmering of the wintry morning's struggling dawn a figure stealthily bending over the wounded man who lay asleep at my side.

The intruder wore the heavy greatcoat and round cap of a Cossack officer, and was evidently searching my comrade's pockets.

"Who are you? What do you want?" I cried in Russian, clutching my revolver.

The man started, withdrew his hand, and stood upright, looking down upon me. For a moment I fixed my eyes upon the statuesque figure, and gazed at him amazed. I am not by any means a nervous man, but there was something weird about the fellow's appearance.

Whether it was due to the suddenness with which I had discovered him, or whether some peculiar phenomenon was caused by his presence, I was unable to determine.

I remember asking myself if I were really awake, and becoming convinced that I was in possession of all my faculties.

"Speak!" I said sternly. "Speak—or I'll fire!"

Raising the weapon, I waited for a moment.

The figure remained motionless, facing the muzzle of the pistol unflinchingly.

Again I repeated my challenge. There was, however, no reply.

I pulled the trigger.

In the momentary flash that followed I caught a glimpse of the face of the intruder. It was that of a woman!

She was young and beautiful. Her parted lips revealed an even row of tightly-clenched teeth, her dark eyes had a look of unutterable horror in them, and her cheeks were deathly pale.

It was the most lovely face I had ever gazed upon.

Its beauty was perfect, yet there was something about the forehead that struck me as peculiar.

The thick dark hair was brushed back severely, and high up, almost in the centre of the white brow, was a curious mark, which, in the rapid flash of light, appeared to be a small but *perfectly-defined bluish-grey ring*!

As I fired, the arm of the mysterious visitor was raised as if to ward off a blow, and in the hand I saw the gleam of steel.

The slender fingers were grasping a murderous weapon—a long, keen surgeon's knife, the blade of which was besmeared with blood.

Was I dreaming? I again asked myself. No, it was not a visionary illusion, for I saw it plainly with my eyes wide-open.

So great a fascination did this strange visitant possess over me, that I had been suddenly overcome by a terrible dread that had deprived me of the power of speech. My tongue clave to the roof of my mouth.

I felt more than ever convinced that there must be something supernatural about the silent masquerader.

In the dim light the puff of grey smoke from the revolver slowly curled before my eyes, hiding for a few seconds the singularly-beautiful countenance.

When, however, a moment later, the veil had cleared, I was amazed to discover that the figure had vanished.

WILLIAM LE QUEUX

My hand had been unsteady.

Grasping my revolver firmly, I sprang to my feet and rushed out of the tent. While gazing quickly around, a Cossack sentry, whose attention had been attracted by the shot, ran towards me.

"Has a woman passed you?" I asked excitedly, in the best Russian I could muster.

"A woman! No, sir. I was speaking with Ivan, my comrade on duty, when I heard a pistol-shot; but I have seen no one except yourself."

"Didn't you see an officer?"

"No, sir," the man replied, leaning on his Berdan rifle and regarding me with astonishment.

"Are you positive?"

"I could swear before the holy *ikon*," answered the soldier. "You could not have seen a woman, sir. There's not one in the camp, and one could not enter, for we are exercising the greatest vigilance to exclude spies."

"Yes, yes, I understand," I said, endeavouring to laugh. "I suppose, after all, I've been dreaming;" and then, wishing the man good-morning, I returned to the tent.

It was, I tried to persuade myself, merely a chimera of a disordered imagination and a nervous system that had been highly strained by constant fatigue and excitement. I had of late, I remembered, experienced curious delusions, and often in the midst of most exciting scenes I could see vividly how peaceful and happy was my home in London, and how anxiously yet patiently my friends and relatives were awaiting my return from the dreaded seat of war.

On entering the tent, I was about to fling myself down to resume my rest, when it occurred to me that my wounded comrade might require something. Apparently he was asleep, and it seemed a pity to rouse him to administer the cooling draught the surgeon had left.

Bending down, I looked into his face, but could not see it distinctly, for the light was still faint and uncertain. His breathing was very slight, I thought; indeed, as I listened, I could not detect any sound of respiration. I placed my hand upon his breast, but withdrew it quickly.

My fingers were covered with blood.

Striking a match and holding it close to his recumbent figure, my eyes fell upon a sight which caused me to start back in horror. The face was bloodless, the jaw had dropped; he was dead!

There was a great ugly knife-wound. Captain Alexandrovitch had been stabbed to the heart!

At that moment the loud rumble of cannon broke the stillness, and a second later there was a vivid flash of light, followed by a terrific explosion. The redoubts of Plevna had opened fire upon us again, and a shell had burst in unpleasant proximity to my tent. The sullen roar of the big guns, and the sharp rattle from the rifle-pits, quickly placed us on the defence.

Bugles sounded everywhere, words of command were shouted, there was bustle and confusion for a few minutes, then every one sprang to his post, and our guns recommenced pouring their deadly fire into the picturesque little town, with its two white minarets, its domed church, and its flat-roofed houses, nestling in the wooded hollow.

With a final glance at my murdered comrade, I hastily buckled on my traps, reloaded my revolver, and, taking a photograph from my pocket, kissed it. Need I say that it was a woman's? A moment later, I was outside amid the deafening roar of the death-dealing guns. Our situation was more critical than we had imagined, for Osman, believing that he had discovered a weak point in the girdle of Muscovite steel, was advancing, notwithstanding our fire. A terrible conflict ensued; but our victory is now historical.

We fought the Turks hand to hand, bayonet to bayonet, with terrible desperation, knowing well that the battle must be decisive. The carnage was fearful, yet to me there was one thing still more horrible, for throughout that well-remembered day the recollection of the mysterious murder of my friend was ever present in my mind. Amid the cannon smoke I saw distinctly the features of the strange visitant. They were, however, not so beautiful as I had imagined. The countenance was hideous. Indeed, never in my life have I seen such a sinister female face, or flashing eyes starting from their sockets in so horrible a manner.

But the most vivid characteristic of all was the curious circular mark on the forehead, that seemed to stand out black as jet.

THREE MONTHS AFTERWARDS, ON A rainy, cheerless March afternoon, I arrived at Charing Cross, and with considerable satisfaction set foot once again upon the muddy pavement of the Strand. It is indeed pleasant to be surrounded by English faces, and hear English voices, after a long period of enforced exile, wearying work, and constant uncertainty as to whether one will live to return to old associations and acquaintances. Leaving my luggage at the station, I walked down to the office in Fleet Street to report myself, and having received the welcome of such of the staff as were about the premises at that hour, afterwards took a cab to my rather dreary bachelor rooms in Russell Square.

My life in London during the next few months was uneventful, save for two exceptions. The first was when the Russian Ambassador conferred upon me, in the name of his Imperial master the Tzar, a little piece of orange and purple ribbon, in recognition of a trifling accident whereby I was enabled to save the lives of several of his brave Sibirsky soldiers. The second and more important was that I renounced the Bohemian ease of bachelorhood, and married Mabel Travers, the girl to whom for five years I had been engaged, and whose portrait I had carried in my pocket through so many scenes of desolation and hours of peril.

We took up our residence in a pretty bijou flat in Kensington Court, and our married life was one of unalloyed happiness. I found my wife amiable and good as she was young and handsome, and although she moved in a rather smart set, there was nothing of the butterfly of fashion about her. Her father was a wealthy Manchester cotton-spinner, who had a town-house at Gloucester Gate, and her dowry, being very considerable, enabled us to enter society.

On a winter's afternoon, six months after our marriage, I arrived home about four o'clock, having been at the office greater part of the day, writing an important article for the next morning's issue. Mabel was not at home, therefore, after a while, I entered the diningroom to await her. The hours dragged on, and though the marble clock on the mantelshelf chimed six, seven, and even eight o'clock, still she did not return. Although puzzled at her protracted absence, I was also hungry, so, ringing for dinner to be served, I sat down to a lonely meal.

Soon afterwards Mabel returned. She dashed into the room, gazed at me with a strange, half-frightened glance, then, rushing across, kissed me passionately, flinging her arms about my neck, and pleading to be forgiven for being absent so long, explaining that a lady, to whose "At Home" she had been, was very unwell, and she had remained a couple of hours longer with her. Of course I concealed my annoyance, and we spent the remainder of the evening very happily; for, seated before the blazing fire in full enjoyment of a good cigar and liqueur, I related how I had spent the day, while she gave me a full description of what she had been doing, and the people she had met.

Shortly before eleven o'clock the maid entered with a telegram addressed to Mabel. A message at that hour was so extraordinary, that I took it and eagerly broke open the envelope.

It was an urgent request that my wife should proceed at once to the house of her brother George at Chiswick, as something unusual had happened. We had a brief consultation over the extraordinary message, and as it was late, and raining heavily, I decided to go in her stead.

An hour's drive in a cab brought me to a large red-brick, ivy-covered house, standing back from the road, and facing the Thames near Chiswick Mall. It was one of those residences built in the Georgian era, at a time when the *fetes champetres* at Devonshire House were attended by the King, and when Chiswick was a fashionable country retreat. It stood in the centre of spacious grounds, with pretty serpentine walks, where long ago dainty dames in wigs and patches strolled arm-in-arm with splendid silk-coated beaux. The house was one of those time-mellowed relics of an age bygone, that one rarely comes across in London suburbs nowadays.

Mabel's brother had resided here with his wife and their two children for four years, and being an Oriental scholar and enthusiast, he spent a good deal of his time in his study.

It was midnight when the old man-servant opened the door to me.

"Ah, Mr. Harold!" he cried, on recognising me. "I'm glad you've come, sir. It's a terrible night's work that's been done here."

"What do you mean?" I gasped; then, as I noticed old Mr. Travers standing pale and haggard in the hall, I rushed towards him, requesting an explanation.

"It's horrible," he replied. "I—I found poor George dead—*murdered*!"

"Murdered?" I echoed.

"Yes, it is all enshrouded in mystery," he said. "The detectives are now making their examination."

As I followed him into the study, I felt I must collect myself and show some reserve of mental strength and energy, but on entering, I was horror-stricken at the sight.

This room, in which George Travers spent most of his time, was of medium size, with French windows opening upon the lawn, and lined from floor to ceiling with books, while the centre was occupied by a large writing-table, littered with papers.

Beside the table, with blanched face upturned to the green-tinted light of the reading-lamp, lay the corpse of my brother-in-law, while from a wound in his neck the blood had oozed, forming a great dark pool upon the carpet.

It was evident that he had fallen in a sitting posture in the chair

WILLIAM LE QUEUX

when the fatal blow had been dealt; then the body had rolled over on to the floor, for in the position it had been discovered it still remained.

The crime was a most remarkable one. George Travers had retired to do some writing shortly before eight o'clock, leaving his father and his wife together in the drawing-room, and expressing a wish not to be disturbed.

At ten, old Mr. Travers, who was about to return home, entered the room for the purpose of bidding his son good-night, when, to his dismay, he found him stabbed to the heart, the body rigid and cold. The window communicating with the garden stood open, the small safe had been ransacked, the drawers in the writing-table searched, and there was every evidence that the crime was the deliberate work of an assassin who had been undisturbed.

No sound had been heard by the servants, for the murderer must have struck down the defenceless man at one blow.

Entrance had been gained from the lawn, as the detectives found muddy footprints upon the grass and on the carpet, prints which they carefully sketched and measured, at length arriving at the conclusion that they were those of a woman.

They appeared to be the marks of thin-soled French shoes, with high heels slightly worn over.

Beyond this there was an entire absence of anything that could lead to the identification of the murderer, and though they searched long and diligently over the lawn and shrubbery beyond, their efforts were unrewarded.

It was dawn when I returned home, and having occasion to enter the kitchen, I noticed that on a chair a pair of woman's shoes had been placed.

They were Mabel's. Scarcely knowing why I did so, I took them up and glanced at them. They were very muddy, and, strangely enough, some blades of grass were embedded in the mud. Then terrible thoughts occurred to me.

I recollected Mabel's long absence, and remembered that one does not get grass on one's shoes in Kensington.

The shoes were of French make, stamped with the name of "Pinet." They were thin-soled, and the high Louis XV heels were slightly worn on one side.

Breathlessly I took them to the window, and, in the grey light, examined them scrupulously. They coincided exactly with the pair the detectives were searching for, the wearer of which they declared was the person who stabbed George Travers to the heart!

The dried clay and the blades of grass were positive proof that Mabel had walked somewhere besides on London pavements.

Could she really have murdered her brother? A terrible suspicion entered my soul, although I strove to resist it, endeavouring to bring myself to believe that such a thought was absolutely absurd; but at length, fearing detection, I found a brush and removed the mud with my own hands.

Then I walked through the flat and entered the room where Mabel was soundly sleeping. At the foot of the bed something white had fallen. Picking it up, I discovered it was a handkerchief.

A second later it fell from my nerveless grasp. It had dark, stiff patches upon it—the ugly stains of blood!

THE ONE THOUGHT THAT TOOK possession of me was of Mabel's guilt. Yet she gave me no cause for further suspicion, except, indeed, that she eagerly read all the details as "written up" in those evening papers that revel in sensation.

George was buried, his house was sold, and his widow went with her children to live at Alversthorpe Hall, old Mr. Travers' place in Cumberland.

Mabel appeared quite as inconsolable as the bereaved wife.

"Do you believe the police will ever find the murderer?" she asked me one evening, when we were sitting alone.

"I really can't tell, dear," I replied, noticing how haggard and serious was her face as she gazed fixedly into the fire.

"Have—have they discovered anything?" she inquired hesitatingly.

"Yes," I answered. "They found the marks of a woman's shoes upon the lawn."

She started visibly and held her breath.

"Ah!" she gasped; "I—I thought they would. I knew it—I knew—"

Then, sighing, she drew her hand quickly across her brow, and, rising, left me abruptly.

ABOUT TWO MONTHS AFTERWARDS, MABEL and I went down to Alversthorpe on a visit, and as we sat at dinner on the evening of our arrival, Fraulein Steinbock, the new German governess, entered to speak with her mistress.

For a moment she stood behind the widow's chair, glancing furtively at me. It was very remarkable. Although her features bore not the slightest resemblance to any I had ever seen before, they seemed somehow familiar. It was not the expression of tenderness and purity of soul that entranced me, but there was something strange about the forehead. The dark hair in front had accidentally been parted, disclosing what appeared to be *a portion of a dark ugly scar*!

Chancing to glance at Mabel, I was amazed to notice that she had dropped her knife and fork, and was sitting pale and haggard, with her eyes fixed upon the wall opposite.

Her lips were moving slightly, but no sound came from them.

When, on the following morning, I was chatting with the widow alone, I carelessly inquired about the new governess.

"She was called away suddenly last night. Her brother is dying," she said.

"Called away!" I echoed. "Where has she gone?"

"To London. I do hope she won't be long away, for I really can't do without her. She is so kind and attentive to the children."

"Do you know her brother's address?"

She shook her head. Then I asked for some particulars about her, but discovered that nothing was known of her past. She was an excellent governess—that was all.

Twelve months later. One evening I had been busy writing in my own little den, and had left Mabel in the drawing-room reading a novel. It was almost ten o'clock when I rose from my table, and, having turned out my lamp, I went along the passage to join my wife.

Pushing open the door, I saw she had fallen asleep in her little wicker chair.

But she was not alone.

The tall, statuesque form of a woman in a light dress stood over her. The profile of the mysterious visitor was turned towards me. The face wore the same demoniacal expression, it had the same dark, flashing eyes, the same white teeth, that I had seen on that terrible day before Plevna!

As she bent over my sleeping wife, one hand rested on the chair, while the other grasped a gleaming knife, which she held uplifted, ready to strike.

For a moment I stood rooted to the spot; then, next second, I dashed towards her, just in time to arrest a blow that must otherwise have proved fatal.

She turned on me ferociously, and fought like a wild animal, scratching and biting me viciously. Our struggle for the weapon was desperate, for she seemed possessed of superhuman strength. At last, however, I proved victor, and, wrenching the knife from her bony fingers, flung it across the room.

Meanwhile Mabel awoke, and, springing to her feet, recognised the unwelcome guest.

"See!" she cried, terrified. "Her face! It is the face of the man I met on the night George was murdered!"

So distorted were the woman's features by passion and hatred, that it was very difficult to recognise her as Fraulein Steinbock, the governess.

In a frenzy of madness she flew across to Mabel, but I rushed between them, and by sheer brute force threw her back upon an ottoman, where I held her until assistance arrived. I was compelled to clutch her by the throat, and as I forced her head back, the thick hair fell aside from her brow, disclosing a deep, distinct mark upon the white flesh—a bluish-grey ring in the centre of her forehead.

Screaming hysterically, she shouted terrible imprecations in some language I was unable to understand; and eventually, after a doctor had seen her, I allowed the police to take her to the station, where she was charged as a lunatic.

It was many months before I succeeded in gleaning the remarkable facts relating to her past. It appears that her real name was Darya Goltsef, and she was the daughter of a Cossack soldier, born at Darbend, on the Caspian Sea. With her family she led a nomadic life, wandering through Georgia and Armenia, and often accompanying the Cossacks on their incursions and depredations over the frontier into Persia.

It was while on one of these expeditions that she was guilty of a terrible crime. One night, wandering alone in one of the wild mountain passes near Tabreez, she discovered a lonely hut, and, entering, found three children belonging to the Iraks, a wandering tribe of robbers that infest that region.

She was seized with a terrible mania, and in a semi-unconscious state, and without premeditation, she took up a knife and stabbed all three. Some men belonging to the tribe, however, detected her, and at first it was resolved to torture her and end her life; but on account of her youth—for she was then only fifteen—it was decided to place on her forehead an indelible mark, to brand her as a murderess.

It is the custom of the Iraks to brand those guilty of murder;

therefore, an iron ring was made red hot, and its impression burned deeply into the flesh.

During the three years that followed, Darya was perfectly sane, but it appeared that my friend, Captain Alexandrovitch, while quartered at Deli Musa, in Transcaucasia, killed, in a duel, a man named Peschkoff, who was her lover. The sudden grief at losing the man she loved caused a second calenture of the brain, and, war being declared against Turkey just at that time, she joined the Red Cross Sisters, and went to the front to aid the wounded. I have since remembered that one evening, while before Plevna, I was passing through the camp hospital with Alexandrovitch, when he related to me his little escapade, explaining with happy, careless jest how recklessly he had flirted, and how foolishly jealous Peschkoff had been.

He told me that it was an Englishman who had been travelling for pleasure to Teheran, but whose name he did not remember, that had really been the cause of the quarrel, and laughed heartily, with a Russian's pride of swordsmanship, as he narrated how evenly matched Peschkoff and he had been.

That just cost my friend his life, for Darya must have overheard.

Then the desire for revenge, the mad, insatiable craving for blood that had remained dormant, was again aroused; and, under the weird circumstances already described, she disguised herself as a man, and, entering our tent, murdered Alexandrovitch.

On further investigation, I discovered that the unknown English traveller was none other than George Travers, for in one of the sketchbooks he had carried during his tour in the East, I found a well-executed pencil portrait of the Cossack maiden.

Darya's motive in coming to England was, without doubt, one of revenge, prompted by the terrible aberration from which she was suffering.

Mabel, who had refrained from saying anything regarding the murder of her brother, fearing lest her story should appear absurd, now made an explanation. On the night of the tragedy, she was on her way to the house at Chiswick, and, when near the gates, a well-dressed young man had accosted her, explaining that he was an old friend of George's recently returned from abroad, and wished to speak with him privately without his wife's knowledge. He concluded by asking her whether, as a favour, she would show him the way to enter her brother's room without going in at the front door. The story told by the young man seemed quite plausible, and she led him up to the French windows of the study.

Then she left the stranger, and crossed the lawn to go round to the front door, but at that moment the clock of Chiswick church chimed, and, finding the hour so late, she suddenly resolved to return home.

Later, when she heard of the tragedy, she was horrified to discover that she had actually aided the assassin, but resolved to preserve silence lest suspicion might attach itself to her.

She now identified the distorted features of the madwoman as those of the young man, and when I questioned her with regard to the bloodstained handkerchief, she explained how, in groping about the shrubbery in the dark, she had torn her hand severely on some thorns.

THE CLOUD OF SUSPICION THAT had rested so long upon Mabel is now removed, and we are again happy.

The carefully-devised plots and the devilish cunning that characterised all the murderess's movements appeared most extraordinary; nevertheless, in cases such as hers, they are not unheard of. Darya is now in Brookwood Asylum, hopelessly insane, for she is still suffering from that most terrible form of madness,—acute homicidal mania,— and is known to the attendants as "The Woman with a Blemish."

VII

THE SYLPH OF THE TERROR

A h! you in England, here, are always *debonnaire*, while we in Charleroi are always *triste*, always."

The dark-eyed, handsome girl sighed, lying lazily back among the cushions of the boat, allowing the rudder-lines to hang so loosely that our course became somewhat erratic. I had been spending one of the hot afternoons of last July gossiping and drinking tea on the riverside lawn of a friend's house at Datchet, and now at sunset had taken for a row this pretty Belgian whom my hostess had introduced as Cecile Demage.

"Is this your first visit to London?" I asked, noticing she spoke English fluently, but with a pleasing accent.

"Oh no," she replied, laughing. "I have been here already two times. I like your country so very much."

"And you come here for pleasure—just for a little holiday?"

"Yes," she answered, lifting her long lashes for an instant. "Of course I travel for—for pleasure always."

Fixing my eyes upon her steadily, I remained silent, pulling long, slow strokes. The evening was calm and delightful, but the blood-red after-glow no longer reflected on the placid Thames, for already the purple haze was gathering.

"You know many Belgians in London, I suppose?" I said at last.

"Oh dear, no!" she answered, with a rippling laugh, toying with one of her gloves that lay on the cushion beside her. "True, I know some of the people at our Legation; but I come abroad to visit the English, not the Belgians."

"And you have never visited West Hill, Sydenham, mademoiselle?" I asked, resting upon the oars suddenly, and looking straight into her dark, wide-open eyes.

She started, but next second recovered her self-possession.

"No, not to my knowledge."

"And have you never met Fedor Nikiforovitch; has he never addressed you by your proper name, Sonia Ostroff?"

The colour left her face instantly, as she started up with a look of abject terror in her eyes.

"M'sieur is of the Secret Police!" she gasped hoarsely, clenching her hands. "*Dieu!* Then I am betrayed!"

"No," I answered calmly. "I am aware that mademoiselle is an active member of the Narodnaya Volya, but, I, too, am a friend of the Cause;" and I added a word which signifies indivisibility, and is the recognised password of the Circle of desperate Russian revolutionists to which she belonged. It gave her confidence, and she sank back upon the cushions, questioning me how I had recognised her.

"I heard you were masquerading in London," I said; "and among other members of the Circle who are here at the present moment are young Paul Tchartkoff, Sergius Karamasoff, and Ivan Petrovitch."

"But—but who are you, m'sieur, that you should know so much about the Narodnaya Volya? When we were introduced, I failed to catch your name distinctly."

"My name is Andrew Verney, and I am an English journalist."

"Andrew Verney! Ah! of course I have heard of you many times! You were the English newspaper correspondent who, while living at Warsaw, became one of Us, and wrote articles to your journal advocating the emancipation of our country and the inviolability of the individual and of his rights as a man. You assisted us in bringing our case vividly before the English people, and in raising money to carry on the propaganda. But, alas! the iron hand of the Minister of the Interior fell upon you."

"Yes," I said, laughing; "I was expelled with a cancelled passport, and an intimation from the Press Bureau at Petersburg that whatever I wrote in future would not be allowed to enter Russia."

Our boat was drifting, so I bent again to the oars, and rowed back to the lawn of our hostess.

The beautiful girl, who, lolling back upon the saddlebags, commenced to chatter in French about mutual friends in Warsaw, in Moscow, and in Petersburg, was none other than Sonia Ostroff, known to every Nihilist in and out of Russia as "The Sylph of the Terror." Her slim figure, her childish face, her delicate complexion and charming dimples made her appear little more than a girl; yet I well knew how her bold, daring schemes had caused the Tzar Alexander to tremble. The daughter of a wealthy widow moving in the best society in Petersburg, she had become imbued with convictions that had induced her to join the Nihilists. From that moment she had become one of their most active members, and on the death of her mother, devoted all the money she inherited to the Cause. Many were the remarkable stories I had

WILLIAM LE QUEUX

heard of the manner in which she had arranged attempts upon the lives of the Tzar and his Ministers; how, on one occasion, with extraordinary courage, she had taken the life of a police spy with her own hand; and how cleverly she had always managed to elude the vigilance of the ubiquitous agents of the Third Section of the Ministry of the Interior. Yet, as she laughed lightly, and pulled the rudder-line sharply, bringing us up to the steps before our hostess's house, few would have suspected Cecile Demage, the *chic*, flippant daughter of a Belgian mine-owner, to be the same person as Sonia Ostroff, the renowned "Sylph of the Terror," who spent greater part of her time in hiding from the police in the underground cellar of a presumably disused house near the Ekaterinski in Petersburg.

Half an hour later we were sitting opposite each other at dinner, where she shone brilliantly as a conversationalist. Several persons were present who had met her in society in Brussels; but none suspected the truth—I alone held her secret.

When later that night we bade each other farewell at Waterloo Station, she managed to whisper, "I shall be at Fedor's on Thursday night at nine. Meet me there. Do not fail."

"Very well," I replied; and, allowing her well-gloved hand to rest in mine for a moment, she bade me *au revoir*, entered a cab, and was driven away.

As I walked into Fedor Nikiforovitch's handsomely-furnished drawing-room at Sydenham to keep my appointment, my host rose to greet me. He was tall, thin and slightly bent by age. In Warsaw I had known him as an active revolutionist, and, indeed, the men who were with him—Tchartkoff, Petrovitch, and Karamasoff—were a trio of daring fellows, who, alone and unaided, had committed many startling outrages. Several others were in the room, and among them I noticed two ladies, Mascha Karelin and Vera Irteneff, whom I had frequently met at secret meetings of the Circle at Warsaw.

"Sonia told me you were coming," Fedor said gayly. "This is the final council. The attempt will be made to-morrow," he added in a whisper.

"The attempt? What do you mean?" I asked.

"It will all be explained in due course," he said, turning away to greet another member who at that moment arrived.

In a few moments, Sonia, in a striking evening toilet, and wearing a magnificent diamond necklet, entered smiling, being greeted enthusiastically on every hand. We exchanged a few words, then, when every one was seated in silent expectancy, "The Sylph of the Terror" took up a position on the tiger's skin stretched before the hearth. The door having been closed, and precautions taken so that there should be no eavesdroppers at the windows that overlooked the flower-garden at the rear, in clear, distinct tones she addressed the assemblage in Russian as "Fellow-councillors of the Narodnaya Volya." She referred to the manifesto of the Narodnoe Pravo, and said, "Autocracy, after receiving its most vivid expression and impersonation in the reign of the present Tzar, has with irrefutable clearness proved its impotence to create such an order of things as should secure our country the fullest and most regular developments of all her spiritual and material forces." Then, with a fire of enthusiasm burning in her dark, flashing eyes, she referred to the thousands of political prisoners, many of them their own relatives and friends, who had been banished without trial to Siberia, to rot in the dreaded silver mines of Nerchinsk, or die of fever in the filthy *etapes* of the Great Post Road.

"Desperate cases require desperate remedies," she continued, glancing around her small audience. "Hundreds of our innocent comrades are at this moment being arrested in Warsaw, and hurried off to the Trans-Baikal without trial, merely because Gourko desires to curry favour with his Imperial master."

"Shame!" they cried, with one accord.

"He must die," exclaimed Fedor.

"Shall we allow our brothers and our sisters to be snatched from us without raising a hand to save them?" she asked excitedly. "No. Long enough have we been idle. To-morrow, here, in London, we shall strike such a blow for the liberty of Russia that the world will be convulsed."

"All is ready, sister," Fedor observed. "The arrangements for escape are perfect. By midnight to-morrow we shall have separated, and not even the bloodhounds of the Third Section will be able to trace us."

"Then let us see the shell," she said. Walking over to a bookcase, he touched a spring, and part of one of the rows of books flew open, disclosing a secret cupboard behind. The backs of the books were imitations, concealing a spacious niche, from which the Nihilist drew forth a thick volume about seven inches long by five wide, bound in black cloth. It was an imitation of a popular edition of Charles Lamb's works.

The bomb was in the form of a book!

Sonia, into whose delicate hands he gave it, examined it critically, with a grim smile of satisfaction, then placed it carefully upon a little Moorish coffee-stool at her side.

"It is excellently made, excites no suspicion, and reflects the greatest credit upon you, Fedor. You are indeed a genius!" she said, laughing. Then, seriously, she asked, "Is every one present prepared to sacrifice his or her life in this attempt?"

"We are," they answered, with one accord.

"I think, then, that we are all agreed both as to the necessity of this action, as well as to the manner the *coup* shall be accomplished. In order that each one's memory shall be refreshed, I will briefly repeat the arrangements. To-morrow night, punctually at eight o'clock, the man condemned to die will visit the Lyceum Theatre, entering by the private door in Burleigh Street. The person using the shell must stand at the Strand corner of that street, and the blow must be delivered just as the carriage turns from the Strand, so that in the crowd in the latter thoroughfare escape may be easy. It must be distinctly remembered, however, that the personage to be 'removed' will occupy the second carriage—not the first."

"Will he be alone?" asked the dark-bearded ruffianly fellow I knew as Sergius Karamasoff.

"Yes. We have taken due precautions. Come, let us decide who shall deliver the blow." And while Fedor wrote a word on a piece of paper, and folding it, placed it with eleven other similar pieces in a Dresden bowl, Sonia Ostroff continued to discuss where they should next meet after the *coup*. At last it was arranged, upon her suggestion, that they should all assemble at the house of Karamasoff in Warsaw at 9 P.M. on the 21st, thus allowing a fortnight in which to get back to Poland.

The scraps of paper were shuffled, and everyone drew, including myself, for I had taken the oath to the revolutionary section of the Narodnaya Volya, and, being present, was therefore compelled to share the risk. Judge my joy, however, on opening mine and finding it a blank! The person to whom the dangerous task fell made no sign, therefore all were unaware who would make the attempt. The strictest secrecy is always preserved in a Nihilist Circle, so that the members are never aware of the identity of the person who commits an outrage.

But the business of the secret council was over, the cunningly-concealed bomb was removed to a place where it was not likely to be accidentally knocked down, and the remainder of the evening passed in pleasant conversation. I had become fascinated by Sonia's beauty, and when I found myself sitting alone with her in a corner of the room where we could not be overheard, I whispered into her ear words of love and tenderness. She, on her part, seemed to have no aversion to a mild flirtation, and admitted frankly that she had pleasant recollections of the sunset hour upon the Thames.

"Who is the man condemned to death?" I asked presently.

"What! are you unaware?" she exclaimed in surprise. "Why, the Tzarevitch."

"The Tzarevitch? And you intend to murder him?"

She shrugged her shoulders, replying, "We have followed him here because he is not so closely guarded as in Petersburg. If we succeed, there will be no heir-apparent, for the Grand Duke George is already dying in the Caucasus, and the days of the autocrat Alexander are numbered. He will die sooner than the world imagines."

The flippant manner in which she spoke of death appalled me; nevertheless, when I bade her farewell, I was deeply in love with her, and promised to be in the vicinity of the scene of the tragedy on the morrow.

I KNEW ALL THE DETAILS of this desperate plot to kill the Russian heir-apparent—then on a brief visit to London with his *fiancee*—yet I dared not inform the police, for the terrible vengeance of the Circle was always swift and always fatal. Helpless to avert the calamity, I passed the long day in breathless anxiety, dreading the fatal moment when the blow would be struck. By some strange intuition, I felt that my every action was watched by emissaries of the Nihilists, who feared treachery on my part, for, as a journalist, I was personally acquainted with a number of officers at Scotland Yard. Hour by hour I strove to devise some plan by which I might prevent the foul murder that was about to be perpetrated; but, alas! no solution of the problem presented itself. The plans had been laid with such care and forethought, that undoubtedly the Tzarevitch would fall a victim, and Russia would be plunged into mourning.

At length twilight deepened into night, and as I walked from Charing Cross down the noisy, bustling Strand, the gas lamps were already alight, and the *queues* were forming outside the theatres. On passing the steps leading to Exeter Hall, I was startled by a hand being laid upon my arm, and found beside me an elderly woman, poorly-clad, wearing a faded and battered bonnet, with a black, threadbare shawl wrapped around her.

"You have not failed, then?" she exclaimed in low tones, that in an instant I recognised.

"You, Sonia? And in this disguise!" I cried.

"Hush! or we may be overheard!" she said quickly. "The choice fell upon me, but—but I have had a fainting fit, caused by over-excitement, and I cannot trust myself;" and she caused me to walk back and turn up Exeter Street, a short and practically deserted thoroughfare close by.

"Think, are not the risks too great?" I urged. "Why not abandon this attempt?"

"I have sworn to make it," she answered determinedly.

"And the others—where are they?"

"An alarm has been raised. Baranoff, the chief of the Third Section, suspects, and is in London in search of us. We have all left England, with the exception of Karamasoff, who remains to witness the attempt, and make a report to the council."

"And you will risk your life and liberty by endeavouring to strike this murderous blow, of which you do not feel yourself physically capable? For my sake, Sonia, defer the attempt until another occasion."

"I cannot, even though *you* love me;" and her slim fingers tightened upon mine. Then, a second later, she clasped her hands to her forehead, and, reeling, would have fallen, had I not supported her.

"How—how very foolish I am!" she said, a few moments later. "Forgive me." Then, as she steadied herself and strolled slowly by my side, she suddenly asked earnestly—

"Do you really love me, Andrew?"

"I do," I answered fervently.

"Then dare you—dare you, for my sake, Andrew—dare you *throw the bomb*?" she whispered hoarsely.

Her suggestion startled me. I halted amazed.

"I—I could not—I really could not," I stammered.

"Ah! it is as I thought—you do not love me," she said reproachfully. "But it is time I took up my position at the next corner. If I die, it will be because you refused your assistance. Farewell!"

Before I could detain her, she had turned into the Strand, and was lost among the bustling crowd. Hurrying, I overtook her before she gained the corner of Burleigh Street.

"I have changed my mind, Sonia," I said. "Give it to me; I will act in your stead. Fly to a place of safety, and I will meet you in Warsaw on the day appointed."

From beneath her shawl she carefully handed me the bomb. It was heavy, weighing fully eight pounds. Slipping it into the capacious pocket of the covert coat I was wearing, I stood at the street corner. Sonia refused to leave, declaring that she would remain to witness the death of the son of the Autocrat.

Trembling and breathless, I stood dreading the fatal moment, knowing that my pocket contained sufficient picric acid to wreck the whole street.

Seconds seemed hours.

"As soon as you have thrown it, fly for your life," urged Sonia. Then we remained silent in watchful readiness.

Suddenly, almost before we were aware of it, one of the Marlborough House carriages dashed round the corner past us, and drew up before the small door at the rear of the Lyceum. It was an exciting moment. Without hesitation I took out the deadly missile, and none too soon, indeed, for a second later the Tzarevitch's carriage followed, and just as it passed, I hurled it with all my force against the wheels. Turning, I dashed away across to the opposite side of the Strand, and was there overtaken, a few seconds later, by Sonia and Karamasoff.

"It has not exploded!" they panted, in one breath.

"No," I said. "How do you account for it?"

"The tube of acid has not broken," Karamasoff said. "I predicted failure when I saw it. But let us go. Sooner or later a horse will kick it, or a wheel will pass over it, and then—pouf!"

"Farewell," I said, and we hurriedly separated, each going in a different direction, both of my companions momentarily expecting to hear a terrific report.

But they were disappointed, for a quarter of an hour later I dropped Nikiforovitch's bomb into the Thames from Waterloo Bridge, and next day an urchin was rewarded with a shilling for bringing to my chambers a copy of Lamb's works. It was sadly soiled and damaged, but bore on its fly-leaf my name and address. He said he had found it in the gutter in Burleigh Street!

Events have occurred rapidly since that memorable evening. The Tzarevitch, unaware of how near he was to a swift and terrible death, is now Nicholas II of Russia; while the pretty Sonia Ostroff, still in ignorance of how her plot was thwarted, is at the present moment toiling in the gloomy depths of the Savenski mine in Eastern Siberia.

WILLIAM LE QUEUX

VIII

ONE WOMAN'S SIN

F rith Street is the centre of the foreign quarter of London. The narrow, shabby thoroughfare retains, even on the brightest day in summer, its habitual depressing air of grimy cheerlessness; but enveloped in the yellow fog of a November evening, its aspect is unutterably dismal. Its denizens are a very shady colony, mostly the scum of Continental cities, who, owing to various causes, have been compelled to flee from the police and seek a safe asylum in the region between Shaftesbury Avenue and Oxford Street.

In a meagrely furnished sitting-room on the top floor of one of the dingiest houses in this mean street, a young man sat gazing moodily into the fire. He was of foreign appearance, about twenty-six years of age—tall, dark, and rather good-looking. His negligence of attire gave him a dash of the genial good-for-nothing, yet his pale face wore a grave, thoughtful expression, as his chin rested upon his hand in an utterly dejected attitude.

Beside him, with her hand placed tenderly upon his shoulder, stood a tall, fair-haired woman several years his junior. She was eminently beautiful, with delicately-moulded features and soft grey eyes that betrayed an intense anxiety. It was evident that she was not an inhabitant of that dismal quarter, for the hat she wore was of the latest French mode, her cloak, which had fallen unheeded to the floor, was heavily lined with sable, while upon her hand were several fine rings, that gleamed and sparkled in the feeble rays of the solitary candle.

"But, Paul, why cannot you remain? Here in London you are safe," she argued, speaking in French, and bending over him with earnestness.

"Impossible," he replied, shaking his head gloomily. "It is unsafe to stay here. I must start for America to-morrow."

"And leave me?" she cried. "No, no; we must not part. You know how madly I love you;" and she smoothed his hair tenderly.

"Ah, Adine," he sighed, "Heaven knows, mine will be a bitter sorrow!"

Taking her hand, he raised it reverently to his lips. In the silence that followed, the bells of a neighbouring church chimed slowly.

"Seven o'clock!" she exclaimed suddenly. "I must go at once, for I have invited some people to dine at the hotel. Come now, promise me you will not leave London. You are quite safe here, in this place. Besides, what have you to fear?"

"The police are searching all over Europe for me."

"Do not be discouraged—we shall baffle them yet. I shall return to-morrow afternoon at four, when we can discuss matters further. Be cheerful for my sake, Paul;" and she bent and kissed him.

"Ah, Adine, you are my only friend," he said brokenly. "I am tired of being hunted from place to place, and have been thinking that away in Mexico or Argentina I might be safe."

"But you are not going. We shall not part," she said decisively.

As she spoke, she picked up her cloak and wrapped it about her. Then, shaking hands with him, and lingering for a moment in his embrace, while he kissed her passionately, she opened the door and passed down the rickety stairs to the street.

Paul Denissoff did not offer to accompany her, but stood listening to her retreating footsteps, afterwards sighing heavily and flinging himself back again into his chair, where he sat staring aimlessly at the meagre fire.

It was nearly midnight. In a cozy and well-furnished private room at the Savoy Hotel, Adine, whose guests had departed, was sitting alone with her slippered feet upon the fender, reading. She had exchanged her dinner-dress for a loose gown of pearl-grey silk, and her hair, unbound, fell in rich profusion about her shoulders. Presently her French maid entered noiselessly, and asked—

"Will mademoiselle require anything more?"

"No, not to-night, Ninette," she replied, glancing up from her novel.

"*Bon soir*, madame," exclaimed the girl, and withdrew.

When she had gone, Adine took a cigarette from her silver case, and, lighting it, lay back in her chair in a lazy, contemplative attitude, watching the blue smoke curl upward. For nearly half an hour she sat engrossed in her own thoughts, when suddenly the door was thrown open. Turning, she saw a middle-aged, well-dressed man, wearing the conventional silk hat and overcoat.

"Colonel Solovieff!" she gasped, jumping to her feet.

"Yes," said the intruder coolly, as he closed the door and turned the key. "I have the honour to bear that name. And you? I need not ask, Madame Adine Orlovski, subject of my Imperial master, the Tzar."

Pale, trembling, and with teeth clenched, she felt in the pocket of her dress, and drew forth something bright and shining. It was a small revolver.

"No, no," exclaimed the colonel, laying his hand upon her arm. "Put away that toy. Remember that I am chief of the English Section of Secret Police, and to shoot me will not be a profitable pastime. I shall not harm *you*."

"Why do you intrude here, at this hour?" she asked indignantly.

"I come—as your friend."

"My friend! *Dieu*! Can you believe that I have forgotten the insult you offered me when we last met? My friend!—you, the chief of the Tzar's spies!" she cried angrily.

"And you, Nihilist and assassin, eh?" added the other, with a sinister grin. "Well, well, *ma belle*, we will not speak of such gruesome subjects as the murder of your husband in Petersburg a year ago."

"My husband?" she gasped. "Have you discovered who murdered him?"

"Ah! then you do not forget the facts? Neither do I. He was found shot through the heart within a hundred yards of his house in the Vosnosenskoi Prospekt. The Third Section of Imperial Police have not been idle, and as a result of their inquiries, a warrant has been issued."

"For whom?"

"For the arrest of the woman who chooses to call herself Adine Orlovski, on a charge of murdering her husband."

"Me?" she cried. "Such imputations are infamous!"

"Pray, don't be alarmed," continued the colonel, speaking in Russian, and taking a cigarette from the case that lay open on the table. He seated himself, and calmly lit it, saying, "Sit down; I wish to talk to you."

Breathless with anxiety, she sank into the nearest chair.

"You see," he began, "it is impossible to escape us. Our agents are everywhere. Outside the hotel at this moment are three officers ready to arrest you—"

"They shall not. I'd—I'd rather kill myself."

"Very well. You have the means; do so," he said, with a brutal laugh.

"Ah!" cried the unhappy woman. "You, the chief of the Tzar's bloodhounds, have tracked me here, and I know that, although I am innocent, it is useless for me to expect or plead for mercy."

"Yes, madame, the warrant from the Ministry of the Interior enables me to hand you over to the English police. When you are charged before the magistrate to-morrow morning, I shall apply for your extradition. That will be your first stage upon that long, straight road which leads to Siberia. Your *dossier* at the bureau is complete. Listen; I will relate the details of your crime—"

"No, no! I do not wish to hear," she said, covering her face with her hands. "I am innocent. I admit that I quarrelled with my husband, but I had no thought of such a horrible deed."

"You confess to the quarrel? Good! Now we may advance a step further," said the colonel, stretching out his legs and contemplating the end of his cigarette. "I have also discovered that you know something about the recent attempt at the Winter Palace—in fact, I have indisputable proof that you are a Nihilist."

"Ah! I understand now the depth of your villainy," she said, with fierce indignation. "The charge of murder is brought against me in order that I may be extradited to Russia and tried as a Nihilist! It is another of your devilish schemes."

"You are shrewd," observed the chief of Secret Police, with a grim smile. "But I ought to indicate that I require to know more of the plans of that highly interesting circle of gentlemen who comprise the Revolutionary Executive Committee; and you are the person to furnish it."

"How can I, when I am not a member of the organisation?"

"To prevaricate is useless. It is only by consenting to become an agent of the Third Section that you can escape arrest and punishment," he said slowly.

"A police agent?" she gasped. "It would mean death!"

"Ah!—so you *are* a Revolutionist! I was not mistaken. Very well, I put it plainer. Either you will enter our service, and, while retaining your connection with the Nihilist Circle at Petersburg, disclose their secrets, or I shall execute the warrant. Remember, the Ministry of Police are liberal, and you will be well paid for your information."

Adine was silent. This man was her enemy, and she saw the deeply-laid plot to secure her conviction and exile to Siberia. The allegations against her of promoting the Nihilist propaganda and taking part in conspiracies were true, and she well knew how easily they could be proved. She had been an active agent in a recent attempt to wreck the Tzar's palace, the discovery of which plot had caused Paul Denissoff's flight from Russia. But, on the other hand, she remembered that with members of the Circle treachery was punishable by death.

"Come, I am awaiting your decision," he said impatiently.

In desperation she asked for time to consider. But he was inexorable, and she saw there was but one course open to her—namely, to become a spy.

"I—I will enter your service," she said at length, in a low, hoarse voice. "I cannot refuse, since you make it the price of my freedom."

"Very well," he exclaimed, with satisfaction. "You will find our Tzar a liberal master, and should occasion arise, you will receive our protection. As for your secret alliance with us, no one will be aware of it except yourself. Let us shake hands, madame—or is it mademoiselle?—upon our agreement."

"No, Colonel Solovieff," she replied, drawing herself up haughtily. "I have sufficient reason for declining that honour. It is enough that I have allied myself with your despicable spies. I must wish you good-night."

"Very well, very well," he said in a tone of annoyance, as he picked up his hat and bowed. "*Au revoir*, madame; we shall meet again before long," he added meaningly, and, turning, he unlocked the door and went out.

"To-night—to-night I am vanquished!" she muttered fiercely between her teeth when he was out of hearing; "but henceforward I shall play a double game; and, *ma foi*! I intend to be victor!"

A YEAR LATER, COLONEL SOLOVIEFF had been recalled from London and appointed chief of the Secret Police of St. Petersburg. His success in discovering Nihilist plots in London and Paris had mainly been due to the information furnished by Adine, therefore he had compelled her to return to the Russian capital and take up her residence in the great mansion that had belonged to her late husband. Her implication in the revolutionary conspiracies had placed her completely in his power, and although forced to obey, she made one stipulation—that Paul Denissoff should be allowed to return to Petersburg unmolested. For a long time the colonel withheld this permission, but at length consented, and the fugitive returned to the woman he loved. He was unaware of Adine's alliance with the police, and she feared to tell him, lest he should despise her. A few members of the revolutionary party living in various parts of Russia had been denounced by her, and the Ministry of the Interior, believing the arrests of great importance, had commended Solovieff in consequence; but, truth to tell, the persons convicted were of the least dangerous type, and she always exercised the utmost caution, lest she should bring to justice any enthusiastic member of the party or compromise herself.

Number 87 Nevski Prospekt was a small, rather dilapidated house of three storeys. The window shutters of the ground and first floors being closed, gave it the appearance of being uninhabited. One apartment on the top floor, however, was furnished as a sitting-room, and was tenanted occasionally by Colonel Solovieff. It would have been folly for Adine to have met the chief of police at her house or at any place where they might be observed; therefore, in order to elude the vigilance of spies, both police and revolutionary, that everywhere abound in the Russian capital, he had taken the house in order to provide them with a secret meeting-place.

One afternoon early in spring, she was standing alone in this room, gazing thoughtfully out of the window, awaiting the man she despised and hated. Though possessing wealth, beauty, and influence, her life had been fraught with much bitterness. While she was yet in her teens, she loved Paul Denissoff, at that time a student at Moscow University; but her mercenary mother had compelled her to marry Orlovski, one of the merchant princes of the capital. For two years they lived together very unhappily, until late one night he was found lying dead in the street, shot by an unknown hand.

Adine mourned for him, but it was scarcely surprising that she felt some secret satisfaction at her freedom; especially when Paul, hearing of her bereavement, sought an interview and expressed his sympathy. Then she was unable to conceal the fact that she still loved him, and their mutual affection was resumed. By her marriage Paul's life had become embittered, and this had caused him to develop into a fearless Terrorist, reckless and enthusiastic in the cause of Russian freedom. When she discovered he was a Nihilist, she at once joined the Circle, rendering considerable pecuniary assistance to the cause, and taking a prominent part in the fierce and terrible struggle between the people and the bureaucracy.

Now, however, as a spy, her position was extremely dangerous, and as she stood looking down into the broad thoroughfare, she was reviewing her past, and vainly trying to devise some means by which she could escape from the web that the detested Solovieff had cast about her.

In a few minutes the man with whom she had an appointment entered.

"Ah! good afternoon," he said, tossing his hat and stick upon a divan, and taking a chair at the table in the centre of the room. "Be seated. I have some news for you. Do you recollect that soon after you consented to assist us, you gave me some information regarding a conspiracy at Moscow?"

Her face twitched nervously as she replied in the affirmative.

"Well, we acted upon your statement, and arrested sixteen of the revolutionists, all of whom have been tried by court-martial and sentenced to the mines. In recognition of your services in this instance, I am directed by my Imperial master, the Tzar, to give you this."

And, taking from his pocket-book a bank-note for five hundred roubles, he handed it to her.

She took it mechanically, scarcely knowing what she did. The touch of the limp paper, however, brought to her mind that it was the wages of her treachery. This filled her with indignation, and her face flushed crimson.

"Have you come to offer me yet another insult, Colonel Solovieff?" she cried. "Can you believe that I have fallen so low as to accept money as the price of the lives of poor wretches who are drawn into your merciless clutches? No, tell His Majesty that he may in future keep his paltry roubles. I do not require them. See how I value the Imperial munificence!"

And, taking the note between her fingers, she tore it into small pieces, which she scattered upon the carpet.

"We are not all so wealthy as yourself, madame," he said, somewhat surprised at her unusual independence. "Yet, after all, your scruples regarding these miserable curs, the Nihilists, amount to no more than mere caprice."

"That may be so," she replied quickly; "but in future, whatever information you require, you will obtain for yourself. My efforts on your behalf have been rewarded by gross insult; therefore I shall refuse to disclose any other revolutionary secrets."

"Pardon me, madame; I have no time to bandy words with you, but your decision is somewhat too hasty. I have discovered that three days hence a desperate attempt is to be made upon the life of His Majesty during the review at Peterhof, and further, that you are implicated in it!"

She started; she had believed her secret safe.

"I have resolved to preserve silence," she said abruptly.

"The plot is a most serious and widespread one," he continued, "and I tell you plainly that if you refuse to inform me where the meeting to arrange the final details will take place, I shall arrest both Denissoff and yourself as Nihilists. You have your choice."

She was nonplussed, and sat twirling the ribbons of her dress with nervous fingers, while he leaned his elbows upon the table, looking at her intently.

"I scarcely think it would be worth your while to refuse," he remarked.

"For myself, I care nothing. I am tired of being your puppet."

"You love Paul Denissoff; surely you will save him from Siberia?"

She hesitated. She saw that to avoid Paul's arrest she would be compelled to sacrifice all the members of the committee to whom the elaborate plot against the autocrat Alexander had been entrusted. She shuddered at the thought of the scandal it would create were she arraigned before a court-martial for conspiracy against the Tzar, and thought of the dreary, lifelong exile that would inevitably follow. In her bewilderment she resolved to secure Paul's freedom at any cost.

"So this is but another illustration of your Satanic cunning," she said at last, with knit brows. "I—I suppose it is imperative that I should betray my friends;" and she sighed heavily.

"Ah! I thought you would not care to bear the consequences of refusal," he exclaimed, smiling at her perplexity.

"You laugh!" she cried, her eyes flashing with anger. "It is true that you hold my destiny in your hands, but take care you do not provoke me to desperation."

"Threats do not become you, madame," he replied coolly. "Tell me, where shall I find these conspirators?"

She paused. She was thinking how she could save her friends.

"You know the Bolshaia Ssattovaia?" she said suddenly. "Well, almost exactly opposite the Commercial Bank there is a small leather-shop, with a large kitchen below. Go there to-morrow night at ten o'clock."

"Not to-night?" asked the chief of police, scribbling a memorandum.

"No; to-morrow."

"Very well," he said, rising and putting on his hat. "I am obliged for your information. *Bon jour*, madame. If I have been a little—a little abrupt, forgive me."

A moment later he had gone.

THE SCENE WAS A WEIRD one. In a low, damp, underground cellar, a dozen men and women were sitting around a table, upon the centre of which a playing-card was pinned by a thin ivory-hilted dagger. A couple of guttering candles shed a feeble light upon the pale, determined countenances of the conspirators, among whom sat Paul Denissoff.

The elderly, wild-haired man who sat at the head of the table was speaking authoritatively, and had been explaining to those assembled, the proposals for the *coup* at Peterhof, a map of the neighbourhood being spread before him.

"And now," he said gravely, "we must draw lots for the removal of the traitor to whom I referred at the opening of our council."

A dead silence followed, while a man who sat on the president's right prepared a number of small folded slips of paper. Upon one of these the president scribbled a name. Then they were placed together in a small box, and each of the revolutionists drew. In addition to the president himself, only the person who drew the paper with the name upon it knew who had been guilty of treachery, while all remained in ignorance of the chosen assassin.

Then the council broke up, arranging to meet on the following night.

At nine o'clock on the next evening, Paul Denissoff, pale-faced and haggard-eyed, entered the hall of the great house of the Orlovskis.

"I must see madame at once," he said to a lackey. "Take me to her."

A few moments later he was ushered along a spacious corridor filled with palms and exotics, through a great white and gold ballroom, and presently admitted into a small, exquisitely furnished little apartment, wherein sat Adine, in a lounge chair, doing fancy needlework.

"Ah, Paul?" she cried, starting to her feet. "Why, what ails you?"

"Hush, Adine," he said hoarsely, when the door had closed. "Some one has denounced you to the executive as a traitor. The council have passed sentence of death, and I—I have drawn the fatal number. You must fly—you must leave Russia at once—to-night—for at midnight I must return here to—*to murder you!*"

"*Dieu!*" she gasped. "Then my secret has been divulged! I confess—it is true, Paul. I have been guilty of double dealing, but it was to save— Hark! Listen!"

There were sounds of voices outside the door, which a moment afterwards was flung open, revealing two ordinary-looking individuals, accompanied by several grey-coated police officers.

"Paul Denissoff," exclaimed one of the detectives, stepping forward, "in the name of our father, the Tzar, I arrest you for conspiracy."

"By Heaven! I'll not go with you. I—"

In a moment he had drawn a revolver and placed himself on the defensive; but a second later the weapon was wrenched from his grasp. Adine, pale and weeping, threw herself between him and his captors, but she was roughly thrust aside, and he was handcuffed and conveyed away to the Police Bureau.

THE ASSIZE COURT OF ST. PETERSBURG was crowded to suffocation, for a great trial of Nihilists was concluding. Paul Denissoff, as a preliminary to his punishment, had been kept in solitary confinement in one of the cells deep down under the fortress of St. Peter and St. Paul. Together with thirty other revolutionists, including those arrested in the Bolshaia Ssattovaia, he was now brought up for sentence. The rays of the afternoon sun were slanting across the court, lighting up the dais whereon sat the grave-looking judge, over whose head hung the golden double-headed eagle, surmounted by an *ikon*, or picture of the Virgin.

Those in court were breathless, for sentence was about to be delivered. Presently the judge spoke.

"Prisoners," he said, addressing the motley row of eager-faced men and women before him, "you have all been found guilty of conspiracy to cause the death of His Imperial Majesty the Tzar. There is but one sentence the *Swod* allows me to pronounce, and it is that you shall be banished and kept at labour at the mines for the remainder of your lives."

Above the sobs and wailing which came from the public portion of the court sounded a shrill, piercing, hysterical shriek. Paul, turning sharply, saw that a poorly-clad woman, sitting in the front row of the spectators, had fainted. Her clothes were common, her hair was parted in the middle and brushed back severely; but, notwithstanding the disguise, he recognised her. It was Adine Orlovski.

TWO YEARS HAD GONE BY. Colonel Solovieff, promoted to the rank of general, had been appointed by the Tzar as Governor of the Asiatic Province of Trans-Baikal.

In the whole of Siberia there is no region more desolate than around the Nerchinsk silver mines of Algachi and Pokrovski. Situated far away in Eastern Siberia, near the Mongolian frontier, and distant five thousand versts from St. Petersburg, there is not a tree or bush to be seen in any direction, and the rolling, snow-clad hills suggest in general contour the immense surges and mounds of water raised by a hurricane. The buildings at the entrance to the Pokrovski mine consist only of a tool-house, a shed for the accommodation of the Cossacks of the guard, and a few log-built cabins occupied by convicts allowed out on licence for good behaviour; while dotted here and there are sentry-boxes, before which stand Cossacks leaning on their rifles.

It is impossible to imagine a more terrible and hopeless existence than that to which Paul Denissoff had been consigned, working all day in the damp, muddy galleries of the mine, and at night trudging through the snow back to the close, foul prison of Algachi. It was, indeed, worse than the life of any pariah dog, for, recognising the hopelessness of the situation, he had given way to that inertness begotten of despair.

He had been toiling with his pick for nearly fourteen hours in the gloom of one of the lower galleries of the mine, when an armed warder came and told him it was time to leave. Casting down his pick, he sighed, and rose from the crouching position in which he was compelled to work. The dim candlelight showed he had aged considerably. The iron fetters upon his feet clanked ominously as he walked, and upon his ragged, mud-stained clothes was stitched the great yellow diamond denoting a life sentence.

Presently prisoner and warder came to the foot of the shaft, and both ascended the rickety ladders which led to the surface. At length they emerged into the light of day, and saw standing before one of the log-sheds a row of silent convicts guarded by Cossacks, waiting to be marched back to prison. Paul walked over and joined them. The wind was biting cold, and snow lay deep upon the road.

Outside the cabin of one of the convicts of the "free command" stood two well-appointed four-horse sleighs; and while the shivering men were wondering who could be travelling in this remote colony, another sleigh came rapidly along the road, preceded by two mounted Cossacks.

The vehicle drew up before the convicts, and its occupant, flinging off the rugs that covered him, stepped out. The men removed their hats and cheered, but Paul remained motionless. He recognised that the traveller was General Solovieff, the governor. Enveloped in a great sable-lined coat, from beneath which his sword trailed in the snow, he walked with difficulty over to where the captain of the Cossacks stood. After a few minutes' conversation, the captain turned and shouted—

"Let the convict Denissoff come here!"

Paul stepped forward and saluted.

"Ah, yes," said Solovieff, when he saw him, "This is the man; I knew him in Petersburg. He is very dangerous, therefore, in future, he is not to go to the mines. Let him remain in the prison always. You understand?"

"Yes, your Excellency," replied the captain, wondering why such additional torture should be heaped on a prisoner so well-behaved; for he was well aware that work in the mine was even preferable to life in the foul, overcrowded prison.

"But, your Excellency," protested Paul, "I have not been mutinous. I—"

"Silence!" thundered the general. "Get back to your place!"

As he turned, two persons confronted him—a man who wore an official uniform with the Imperial eagle upon his cap, and a woman wrapped in a great fur-lined travelling cloak.

The recognition was mutual, and in a moment he was wringing Adine's hand.

Meanwhile the man had stepped forward, and, addressing the Cossack officer, said—

"Captain Yagodkin, we have not met before, my name is Ivan Torsneff, and I am an aide-de-camp of His Majesty, the Tzar."

"Ah, I remember you, Torsneff!" cried the general, stretching forth his hand. "What brings you here, so far from Petersburg?"

"An unpleasant duty, General Solovieff," replied the Tzar's messenger coldly. Taking an official document from the pocket of his greatcoat, he added, "I have here a warrant from His Imperial Majesty, my august master, ordering Captain Yagodkin to release the prisoner Paul Denissoff immediately; and, further, to arrest and detain at hard labour the governor of the Trans-Baikal, General Solovieff."

"What?" cried His Excellency. "You're mad!"

"Captain Yagodkin," continued Count Torsneff, "In the name of the Tzar, I hand the warrant to you. It is in His Majesty's own handwriting—read for yourself."

The Cossack officer opened it eagerly, read it through, and glanced at the Imperial signature and seal. Then, addressing the governor, he said—

"General Solovieff, you are under arrest, by order of the Tzar!"

"What for?"

"It has been proved by an accomplice of yours, one Sergius Baranoff," replied the aide-de-camp, "that you are a murderer—that, with the object of eventually marrying Madame Orlovski, you waylaid and murdered her husband. Afterwards, when she rejected your proposals of marriage, you brought circumstantial evidence to bear and accused her of the crime. In your absence, the case has been tried in Petersburg, and your sentence is hard labour in the mines for life."

A few hours later, Paul and Adine had started on the first stage of their journey back to civilisaticn. They are now married, and live happily in one of those charming villas in the pine forest at Arcachon.

IX

Vogue La Galere!

Yes, yes, this is the very spot! Here the great tragedy of my life was enacted. Twenty-four weary years of my existence have passed, and until this moment I have never summoned sufficient courage to visit it. Ah, Dieu! how all has changed! Paris is herself again.

You may perhaps know the place. Near the Porte de la Muette, a little way down the Boulevard Suchet, in the direction of Passy, the fortifications of the city recommence after the open space which gives access to the Bois. The ponderous walls are the same, though the breaches made by the German shells have been repaired, and the stones on which I tread bear no traces of the men's blood that once made them so slippery. One hundred paces from the corner of the Boulevard there is a steep little path running up the grass-grown mound, beside a railing. Ascend it, and you will find yourself on the top of the great wall, below which, deep down in the fosse, on the outside towards the Bois, there is a well-kept market garden. The only noises on this sunny afternoon are the twittering of birds and the rustling of leaves—different sounds and a different outlook indeed to that which is indelibly impressed upon my memory. All are gone, gone! and I alone remain—aged, infirm, forsaken, and forgotten!

What matters, though I still wear my faded scrap of yellow and green ribbon upon the lapel of my shabby coat—what matters if I am an exile, an outlaw; that here, in Paris, after all these years, I dare not inscribe my proper name in the register? To both friends and enemies I am dead!

As I stand looking away over the market garden, towards the shady wood, a film gathers in my eyes, and I am carried back into the terrible past, to those black, fateful days when France lay helpless under the iron heel of the invader, who had encamped around St. Cloud and Suresnes. Paris—fettered, existing upon black bread and horse-flesh—shivered under an icy mantle. The black branches of the leafless trees over in the Bois stood out distinctly against the grey, stormy sky, and upon the ground snow was lying thickly. Hour after hour, day after day, week after week, we had held those walls, regardless of the hail of shell poured upon us from beyond the trees, and replying with monotonous, unceasing regularity. Hundreds of our gallant comrades were, alas! lying dead; hundreds were in the temporary hospitals established in the neighbouring churches; but we, the survivors—half-starved, with the biting wind chilling our bones, and so weak that our greatcoats felt as heavy as millstones,—resolved, every one of us, to face death and do our duty. We knew well that to hold out much longer would be impossible. In those dark December days the city was starving. Our country had been overrun by the Prussian legions, and sooner or later we must succumb to the inevitable.

The night was dark and moonless, as to and fro I paced on sentry duty. My post was a lonely one, under the strongest portion of the wall, at the point I have already indicated. Away in the direction of Courbevoie there was a lurid glare in the sky, showing that the enemy had committed another act of incendiarism; and now and then the booming of artillery echoed like distant thunder. In our quarter the guns of the enemy had ceased their fire—a silence that we felt was ominous. Under my feet the snow crunched as I marched slowly up and down; and with rifle loaded, and ready for any emergency, I waited patiently for relief, which would come at dawn. As I tramped on, I thought of my home away in the centre of the inert, trembling city; of my young wife, blue-eyed, fair-haired, from whom I had been torn away ere our honeymoon was scarcely over. How, I wondered, was she faring? As an advocate I had been distinctly successful, having been entrusted with quite a number of *causes celebres*; but on the outbreak of war my chances of fortune had been suddenly wrecked, and I had been called upon to serve with the 106th Regiment of Infantry, first under General Chanzy on the Loire, and afterwards taking part in the defence of Paris.

Though now so near the woman I loved, I saw very little of her; indeed, I had not been able to snatch an hour to run home for the past fortnight. Yet, while I trudged on, I knew that one of the truest and best women on earth was awaiting me *au troisieme* in the great old house in the Rue St. Sauveur.

I think that for some time I must have been oblivious to my surroundings, for on turning sharply, my eyes suddenly detected some indistinct object, moving cautiously in the shadow. Something prompted me to refrain from challenging, and, with rifle ready, I quickly hurried to the spot. With a cry of surprise, a man in a workman's blouse sprang forward right up to the muzzle of my gun.

I challenged, and presented my rifle.

"Hold!" he gasped in French, in a low, hoarse tone. "Louis Henault, don't you know me? Have you so soon forgotten your fellow-student, Paul Olbrich?"

The voice and the name caused me to start.

"*You!*" I cried, peering into his face, and in the semi-darkness discovering the scar upon his cheek that he had received in the fencing school at Konigswinter. "You, Paul, my best friend! Alas that you are a Prussian, and we meet here as enemies!"

"As enemies?" he repeated, in a strange, harsh tone. "Yes, Louis, you are right," he added bitterly,—"as enemies."

"Why are you here?" I inquired breathlessly. "Why are you disguised as a French workman? It is my duty to arrest you—to—"

"But you will not. Remember, we were friends beside the Rhine, and we can only be enemies to the outside world. Surely you, of all men, will not betray me!"

"When last I heard of you, two years ago," I said, "you were a lieutenant of dragoons. To-night you are here, inside Paris, disguised."

"To tell the truth," he replied quickly, "it is a love escapade. Let me get away quickly beyond the walls, and no one will know that you have detected me. See, over there," and he pointed to a portion of the wall deep in the shadow. "There is my *fiancee*. I have dared to pass through your lines to rescue her before the final onslaught."

I peered in the direction indicated, and could just distinguish a figure, hidden by a cloak, and closely veiled.

"Quick," he continued; "there is no time for reflection. If you raise an alarm, my fate is sealed; if you allow us to proceed, two lives will be made happy. Do you consent?" Grasping my hand, he pressed it hard, adding, "Do, Louis, for *her* sake!"

Muffled footsteps and the clank of arms broke the quiet. Three officers were approaching.

"Go. May God protect you!" I replied; and, turning sharply, tramped onward in the opposite direction, while my old friend, and the woman he had rescued from starvation, were a second later lost in the darkness in the direction of the Prussian camp.

Scarcely had I taken a dozen paces when there were shouts, followed by shots rapidly exchanged.

"Spies!" I heard one of our men exclaim; "and, *sacre!* they've escaped!"

At that moment the officers who had approached ordered me to halt, and proceeded to question me as to whom I had been speaking with. I admitted that the man was a stranger, and that I had allowed him to pass out of the city. Thus all was discovered, and I was at once arrested as a traitor—as one who had rendered assistance to a Prussian spy!

The penalty was death. The stern, grey-haired general before whom I was taken half an hour later pronounced sentence; and, without ceremony, I was hurried off to execution. Bah! Fate has always been unkind to me. It would have been better had I fallen with four of my comrades' bullets in my breast, than that I should have continued to drag out an existence till to-day. But the bombardment had recommenced vigorously; and as I was being led along, a shell fell close to my escort, and, bursting, killed two of the poor fellows, and demoralised the rest.

I saw my chance, and darted away. A moment later, I was lost among the trees.

THREE HOURS LATER.

Breathlessly I mounted the long flights of stairs that led to my home, and opened the door with my key. Entering our little salon, I looked around. In the cold, grey light of dawn, the place looked unutterably cheerless, and the thunder of the guns was causing the windows to rattle. Passing quickly into the bedroom, I found the ceiling open to the sky, and a huge gap in the wall A shell had fallen, and completely wrecked it.

"Rose!" I cried. "Rose, I have returned."

There was no response. Another roar like the roll of thunder, and the whole place vibrated, as though an earthquake had occurred.

Where was Rose? I dashed back into the salon, and there, upon a table, I found a letter addressed to me in her familiar hand. Tearing it open, I read eagerly the three brief lines it contained, then staggered back, as if I had received a blow. A second later, I felt conscious of the presence of some one at my elbow; and, turning, found Mariette, our maid-of-all-work.

"My wife—where is my wife?" I gasped.

"Madame has gone, m'sieur," the girl replied in her Gascon accent. "Last night a man called for her, and she went out, leaving a note for you."

"A man?" I cried. "Describe him. What was he like?"

"I only caught one glimpse of him, m'sieur. He was fair, and had a long red scar across his cheek."

"*A scar?*" I shrieked in dismay, as the terrible truth dawned suddenly upon me. Rose, whom I had first met in Cologne, when a student on the Rhine-bank, had told me that I was not her first love; and now I remembered that she had long ago been acquainted with my fellow-student, Paul Olbrich.

It was my own wife whom I had assisted to elope with my enemy!

Ah! time has not effaced her memory. My sorrow is still as bitter to-day as it was in that cold December dawn, with the horrors of war around me. My life has become soured, and my hair grey. Since that eventful night, I have wandered in strange lands, endeavouring to stifle my grief; for, still under sentence of death as a spy, I have been an exile and an outlaw until to-day.

What, you ask, has become of *her*?

Far away, in a secluded valley in the Harz, under the shadow of the mystic Brocken, there is a plain white cross in the village burying-ground, bearing the words, "Rose Henault, 1872."

My enemy, Paul Olbrich, a year after the war had ended, succeeded to the family title and estates; and to-day he is one of the most prominent men in Europe, and acts as the diplomatic representative of Germany at a certain Court that must be nameless.

Truly, Fate has been unkind to me. To-day, for the first time, I have taken my skeleton from its cupboard. Would that I could bury it forever!

X

Fortune's Fool

I am no longer myself. I vanished involuntarily. Truth to tell, I was befooled by Fortune.

As confidential messenger in the service of the Bank of France, it was my duty to convey notes and bullion to various European capitals, and so constantly did I travel between London and Paris, and to Rome, Berlin, and Vienna, that my long journeys became terribly irksome, and I longed for rest and quiet. There is much excitement and anxiety in such a life, when one is entrusted with large sums of money which are impossible to hide in one's pocket.

In the year 1883, England, as is frequently the case, was remitting a quantity of gold coin to France, and consequently, during the month of June, I was making two, and sometimes three, journeys between Paris and London weekly. Incessant travelling, such as this, soon wearies even those inured to long railway journeys, especially if one very often has to arrive in London in the morning only to leave again the same night. A long trip, say to the Austrian or Turkish capitals, was much more to my taste than the wearying monotony of the Dover-Calais route, and the inevitable turmoil between Paris and the English metropolis.

One warm night—although excessively tired, having arrived in London at an early hour that morning—I was compelled to return, and left Charing Cross by the mail train at half-past eight. I had with me a box from the Bank of England containing a large quantity of bullion. As far as Dover I was alone, smoking and dozing over a newspaper, but when I alighted on the pier, the weather had changed. It rained in torrents, and a violent wind was blowing in a manner that was indicative of a "dirty" night.

My expectations in this respect proved correct, and I was glad to arrive at Calais, where I selected an empty first-class compartment, bade the porter deposit my weighty box on the seat, and, wrapping myself comfortably in my travelling rug, settled myself for the remainder of the journey. While such a quantity of gold was in my possession, I dared not sleep, yet, fatigued as I was, I experienced great difficulty in keeping awake. It was always possible that while coin was in my custody

I might be watched and followed by thieves, therefore a loaded revolver constantly reposed in my pocket ready for an emergency.

Few persons were travelling that night, and I was fortunate in having the compartment to myself as far as Abbeville. Then there entered two well-dressed Frenchmen, who, after scrutinising me rather closely, sank into opposite corners of the carriage. Seldom I felt uneasy regarding fellow-travellers; nevertheless, I confess that as I looked at them, I felt a strange, vague shadow of distrust. Instinctively I felt for my revolver, assuring myself that it was ready if required. Somehow I had a suspicion that the men had been on board the Channel boat, and were following me for some evil purpose. But they sat opposite one another smoking, occasionally indulging in conversation, though always keeping their faces concealed as much as possible from the pale, flickering rays of the lamp overhead.

As we sped south, I became more fully convinced that they meant mischief. Looking at my watch, I found that in twenty minutes we should be at Amiens, and determined to change into another carriage there. Patiently I sat, gazing out of the window watching the grey streak of dawn break over the low, distant hills, when suddenly I felt a terrible crushing blow on the top of my skull.

At the same moment I drew forth my revolver and pulled the trigger. Then a darkness fell upon me, and I remember nothing more.

THE SENSATION WAS HORRIBLE; THE pain excruciating. It seemed as though a thousand red-hot needles were being thrust into my brain.

Slowly the terrible throbbing in my head abated, and I found myself seated in an armchair in a well-furnished, though unfamiliar, drawing-room. It was lit by tiny electric lamps, shaded with canary silk; and, as I gazed round in abject astonishment, I noticed a pretty fernery beyond, which looked like a mermaid's grotto in the depths of the sea, so dense was the mass of dimly-illuminated greenery.

My first thoughts were of my charge, and I felt for my pouch, in which I had carried a bundle of bank-notes.

It was not there! Placing my hand upon my chin, I was startled to find that I had a beard, while on the previous night I had been clean shaven! And the box of bullion—where was that?

I started to my feet, and as I did so, my figure was reflected in a long mirror. I staggered back in dismay, for, although last night I was a sprightly and spruce young man of thirty, my hair was now turning grey, and my face so aged and wrinkled that I could scarcely recognise myself!

Where was I? What could it all mean?

I saw a bell, and rang it hastily.

My summons was quickly answered by a sharp-featured man, who was evidently not a servant.

"Tell me, who brought me here? Whose house is this?" I demanded.

He gazed at me, open-mouthed, in astonishment.

"I—er—You're not well, sir, I think. This is your own house."

"Mine?" I cried incredulously. "Nonsense. Who are you, pray?"

"I'm your secretary," he replied, adding, "I—I'll return in a moment;" and then, in evident alarm, he disappeared.

I had no time to reflect upon the mystery of the situation before there entered a tall, beautiful woman, of what might be termed the Junoesque type, attired in a handsome dinner-gown.

"Why, my dear, whatever have you been saying to Norton? You've quite frightened him," she exclaimed, laughing. "How is it that you're not dressed? You remember we promised to dine with the Websters to-night."

"I—I confess I don't understand you, madam," I gasped, for my brain was in a whirl, and everything seemed in maddening confusion. The pain in my head was intense.

"What's the matter? What has happened?" she cried in alarm. "Don't you recognise me—Lena, your wife?"

"My wife?" I gasped, astounded. "No, I've never seen you before. It's some trick. Where is the box—the box that was with me in the train?"

Her look of distress deepened, as she said, "Calm yourself, my dear. You are not well, and must have advice."

"I want none," I replied hotly. "I desire nothing beyond the box. These are not my clothes," I said, glancing in puzzled confusion at the coat I wore. "Where are mine?"

"I don't comprehend your meaning," said the handsome woman who called herself my wife. "Your mind must be wandering, Harry."

"That's not my name. I am Charles Deane."

"No, no, dear," she cried. "You are under some strange delusion. What can have happened to you? You are Henry Medhurst, and I am Lena Medhurst, your wife."

"Where and when did you marry me, pray?"

"In Cape Town, five years ago."

"In Cape Town? And where are we now?"

"This is your house, situate, I think, to be exact, two and a half miles from Johannesburg. Is there anything else you desire to know?" she added, with a smile, half inclined to believe that I was joking.

The crowd of thoughts and feelings that burst upon my mind was indescribable. Was I still myself, or was it all a delusion?

No. It was a stern reality; a deep, inexplicable mystery.

"I married you five years ago, you say. Then what year of grace is this?"

"Come," replied my wife, "such fooling is out of place, dear. You know as well as I that it is 1893."

"What!" I cried, feeling myself grow rigid in amazement. "Yesterday was ten years ago!"

I was undoubtedly wide awake and sensible, but that I was really myself I began to doubt. I struggled to comprehend the situation, but failed. How I came to be in South Africa, the possessor of such a mansion, the husband of such a wife, was a problem beyond solution. I felt light-headed, for the horrible suspense was goading me into a frenzy of madness.

"There must be some—some serious mistake," I said calmly. "I've never had the pleasure of setting eyes upon you before this evening, and am utterly at a loss to understand who or what I am."

She regarded me with a terrified expression; her face suddenly blanched, and she would have fallen, had I not caught her and placed her upon the settee.

Ringing the bell again, a maid-servant answered my summons.

"Your mistress has fainted. Call some one to her assistance," I said; and then I proceeded to explore the house. It was a splendid modern mansion, and by the bright moonlight I discerned that it was surrounded by a well-kept lawn and clumps of fine old trees.

I was utterly unable to realise that the journey to Paris had been made ten years before; nevertheless, my aged appearance, my beard, the fact of my marriage, and my apparent opulence, all combined to confirm her statement. In vain I tried to recollect the incidents of that memorable night; but, beyond the knowledge that I received a terrible blow, I could remember nothing.

Pacing in distraction the broad terrace that ran before the house, I suddenly heard footsteps behind me. Turning, I confronted the man who called himself my secretary.

"Griffiths, the manager of Pike's Reef, has just arrived from Pretoria, and wishes to see you on important business, sir."

"To see me? What for?"

"He desires instructions regarding the Reef. They've struck the lead at last, and the crushings show it to be one of the richest veins in the Randt. Shall I bring him to you?"

"No," I replied savagely; "I want to be alone. I haven't the slightest notion of what you're talking about."

"Surely you know Griffiths, sir? He used to manage your old mine, the Bellefontaine, and is now in charge at Pike's Reef."

"I don't know him, and have no desire to make his acquaintance. Send him away," I said abruptly.

The man, who seemed puzzled, hesitated for a moment, and, after muttering some words in an undertone, re-entered the house.

For nearly half an hour I had remained alone, until the maid appeared, saying, "Mistress would like to see you in the drawing-room, sir."

I obeyed the summons, and on entering the room, found the woman who called me husband seated on a low chair, while near her stood a short, stout old gentleman, in a frock-coat of rather ancient cut, and wearing gold-rimmed pince-nez.

"Ah, my dear Medhurst!" exclaimed the man, greeting me effusively. "How are you this evening?"

"I haven't the pleasure of knowing you, sir," I said indifferently.

"You don't know Dr. Beale? Come, come, this won't do at all," he said, smiling.

I assured him that I had never set eyes upon him before, and went on to explain how I had been travelling to Paris and suddenly struck insensible, only to regain consciousness and find myself in Africa—rich, married, and ten years older.

The doctor listened with grave attention, and subsequently we entered upon a long and rather heated discussion. All I wanted to discover was how I came to be there.

"Monomania, evidently," observed the doctor in a low voice, when we had been talking for some time. "It develops frequently into the most violent form of madness. He will have to be kept in seclusion and watched."

Again I resented the imputation that I was going insane, to which the medical luminary replied, "Very well, my dear fellow, very well. We will believe what you say. Calm yourself; for your wife is nervous and weak, remember."

I turned away disgusted. All my efforts to explain the remarkable facts had only been met with incredulity by the idiotic, soft-spoken old doctor, who undoubtedly imagined I was mad.

In desperation I strode out of the house, and spent the night in wandering about the grounds, and walking aimlessly through unfamiliar roads, subsequently sitting down upon the fallen trunk of a tree, where I fell asleep.

When I retraced my footsteps, the bright morning sun was glinting through the foliage of the dense wood that seemed to almost surround the house.

From a servant I learnt that my *soi-disant* wife was too unwell to leave her room; and as I wandered through the place, I entered one apartment which was evidently a study—my own, possibly. Glancing round at the books, the two great iron safes, and the telephone instruments, I seated myself at the littered writing-table. Turning over the papers before me, I saw they related to mining enterprises involving large sums. Many of them were evidently in my handwriting, but the signatures were "Henry Medhurst," and the note-paper bore the heading, "Great Bellefontaine Gold Mines, Offices, 127 Commissioner Street, Johannesburg."

Upwards of an hour I sat plunged in thought, bewildered by the events of the past few hours. I felt I must make some strenuous effort to solve the enigma, and account for the intervening ten years that I had lost. I could not have been asleep in the manner of the legendary Rip Van Winkle, but must have been existing during the period. Yet where did I live? And how?

It seemed clear from the doctor's words that if I remained, I should be placed under restraint as an imbecile. Therefore the thought suggested itself that I should return to Europe, and endeavour to find out what befell me on that midnight journey. Recollecting that I should require funds, I searched the drawers of the writing-table, and found a cash-box, in which was nearly four hundred pounds in gold and notes. This was sufficient for the journey; and, with a feeling of joy, I transferred it to my pockets, and prepared for departure.

A few hasty lines I wrote to my self-styled wife, informing her of my intention, and stating that I should return as soon as I had gained the information necessary to restore my peace of mind. Afterwards I went to my room, crammed a few necessaries into a travelling-bag, and, without uttering a word of farewell, left the City of Gold *en route* for England.

Arrived in London, I set about tracing my career; but from the outset I found it a task fraught by many difficulties. I must have altered considerably in personal appearance during my absence, for none of my friends recognised me. There was but one agency that seemed likely to render me assistance, namely, the Press. The files of the *Times* and *Telegraph* for 1883 I searched diligently, but gleaned nothing from them. Indeed, I spent several weeks in looking through various daily and weekly papers, published about the time of my fatal journey, without result, until one day it occurred to me that the French Press might aid me. Accordingly, I went to Paris, and on the following day called at the office of the *Gaulois*, where I obtained the file for the year I required. Turning to the paper for the day following my sudden oblivion, my eye fell upon the headline, "Terrible Accident on the Northern Railway." Eagerly I read and reread every word, for here was what seemed a clue to the mystery.

It appeared that the train in which I had travelled, when approaching Longpre, ran into some trucks, and was completely wrecked, seven persons being killed and about twenty injured. In a first-class compartment two passengers were discovered, one of whom had among his luggage a box containing a large sum in English gold and notes. Neither men had been injured by the accident; but one, presumably, in order to obtain possession of the money, had shot his fellow-traveller dead, and was making off with his booty when he was apprehended, and brought to Paris.

In the papers of following days I found a report of the examination before the Juge d'instruction, and the subsequent trial before the Assize Court of the Seine. According to the newspaper accounts, the man charged with wilful murder was young and well-dressed, but seemed enveloped in mystery, inasmuch as he conducted himself strangely, refusing to give his name or any account of himself, and preserving an immutable silence throughout the many days the case lasted. Judging from the prominence given to the report, the trial must have been a celebrated one, and considerable excitement was created in the French capital, owing to the fact that several prominent members of the medical profession, who had examined the accused, agreed that he was suffering from some strange mental affection, the precise nature of which they were unable to discover. It was owing to this that the culprit escaped the guillotine, being sentenced to hard labour for life, and transportation to the penal colony of New Caledonia.

Which was I, the murderer or the murdered?

I felt confident I was one or the other. Therefore, I resolved to find out whether this mysterious convict was still alive; and if so, to seek an explanation from him. The thought occurred to me that an official in the Prisons Department, whom I had known, might be able to furnish me with the information. After some difficulty I discovered him, but he had long ago retired into private life. So entirely had my personal appearance changed, that he did not recognise me. Therefore, by representing that I was an English solicitor, anxious to discover a next-of-kin, and offering to pay handsomely for the investigation, I prevailed upon him to seek an interview with the chief of the department, and ascertain whether the convict was still living.

When I called a few days later, he placed in my hands a memorandum signed by the chief, certifying that after two years at La Nouvelle—as the French prison island is termed,—prisoner Number 8469, committed for life for murder, had effected his escape by means of an open boat in company with Jean Montbazon, who had been convicted of forging Spanish bonds. Both were known to have landed on the Queensland coast after a perilous voyage; but they had disappeared before the Australian police were communicated with, and all efforts to trace them had been futile. Having, however, been employed in the Government mines near Noumea, it was expected that they had obtained work in one of the remote mining districts, where they could effectively hide until the search was over.

To find this man Montbazon was no easy task, but if I chanced to be successful, he might, I thought, tell me something of his whilom comrade in adversity.

I was puzzled how to proceed, but at length resorted to advertising as the only expedient. In the chief French and Colonial newspapers I caused to be inserted a brief paragraph addressed to "Jean Montbazon, late of Noumea," stating that his companion upon the voyage from New Caledonia to Australia wished particularly to meet him, and giving my address at the Table Bay Hotel, Cape Town, whither I proceeded. Patiently I awaited a reply, but although I had spent a large sum upon the advertisement, it apparently failed to reach the man whose acquaintance I desired to make.

For many weeks I remained at the hotel, feeling no desire to return to Johannesburg until I had cleared up the mystery and accounted for my lost identity. Times without number I was tempted to relinquish the effort to trace my past, yet with sheer, dogged perversity, I remained and hoped.

At last my patience was rewarded, for one evening, while I was sitting on the balcony of the hotel, enjoying a cigar in the starlight, the waiter brought me a visitor.

Judge my dismay when I recognised the face of my secretary.

"Well, old fellow," he exclaimed familiarly, "and what means all this confounded mystery?"

I sat speechless in amazement.

"I saw the advertisement in the *Cape Times*, and, concluding that something was wrong, came down here. What is it?" he continued, sinking lazily into a chair by my side.

"The advertisement?" I gasped. "I—I don't understand you."

"Your advertisement was addressed to Jean Montbazon, your humble and obedient servant, who shared your lot at La Nouvelle, and who escaped with you."

"What?" I cried. "Is that true?"

"I think, *mon cher ami*, you must have taken leave of your senses, as madame declares you have. Come, now, what's the matter?"

"Are—are you really Jean Montbazon?"

"That's my baptismal cognomen, though Fred Norton suits me better just now."

"Look here," I said earnestly: "I admit I'm not quite myself; indeed, I have forgotten everything. Tell me how we escaped, and why I am so rich, while you are my secretary."

The man looked at me incredulously, remarking, "*Ma foi*! I thought you were a bit vacant before you left Johannesburg so mysteriously, but you now seem stark mad. It would take a long time to recount all our adventures, and some would be rather unpleasant reminiscences. You were sent to penal servitude for life for murder, and I for forgery. We were pals in the same labour-gang, and one day, finding an open boat upon the beach, we resolved to escape, and embarked. In the boat was a keg of water and a barrel of biscuits, which sufficed to keep body and soul together until, after a terrible voyage lasting many days, we ran ashore near Port Curtis, in Queensland. Having regained our freedom, we tramped to the gold diggings, and worked together for about a year. You had extraordinary luck, and soon became rich, while I was often obliged to exist upon your charity. In a year, however, an unfortunate incident occurred at our camp at Gum Tree Gulch. A man who was known to have a quantity of dust in his belt was found dead, with an ugly wound upon his head; and, in consequence of this, Australia became too warm for you and I. Therefore we left the camp hurriedly one night, without wishing adieu to our comrades, and came here, to South Africa, to try our luck. As usual, your good fortune did not desert you. Already rich, you bought some big claims in the Randt, and worked them with almost incredible results. Then the boom came."

"And how did that affect me?"

"You had previously married a wealthy woman before the gold fever set in. When the boom came, you sold both her property and yours at such prices that within three weeks you were almost a millionaire."

"What am I now?" I asked, amazed at this remarkable story.

"You are owner of two of the richest gold workings in the Transvaal, and I—always a Lazarus—am your confidential secretary. Most confidential, I assure you," he added, smiling. "The master a murderer; the servant a forger!"

HAVING THUS FILLED UP THE long blank in my memory, I did not rest until I had satisfactorily accounted for the events of that fateful night. Subsequently I discovered that the violent blow on my head, received in the accident, had produced such an effect on my brain as to render oblivious all the events of my past. From that moment I commenced a second life. One of my fellow-passengers, noticing my injury, was endeavouring to steal the box of bullion, when I shot him dead with my revolver. Afterwards, when I had recovered consciousness, I opened the box, and, secreting part of the money in my pockets, tried to get away unobserved. But I was arrested, tried for murder, and transported. The rest is known.

At my trial I refused to give any account of myself, for the simple reason that I remembered nothing. My mind was an absolute blank. I had lived an entirely different life for ten years, until I accidentally struck my head a violent blow against the corner of a mantelshelf in my drawing-room, causing the memory of my earlier life to return as suddenly as it had fled, and thus leaving a gap of ten years for me to fill.

Mine was an extraordinary case; but, as I afterwards discovered, my duality of brain was by no means unprecedented. Such vagaries of the mind, although rare, are known to medical science.

WILLIAM LE QUEUX

When, a week afterwards, I returned to Johannesburg—that dusty, noisy City of Mammon—Lena welcomed me warmly. The same evening, after I had explained to her the cause of my sudden disappearance and apparent insanity, she went to her room, and on her return handed me a faded blue envelope, secured by the official seal of the Bank of England.

"This," she said, "you asked me to keep for you, on the day we were married."

I glanced at the superscription, and recognised the handwriting. It contained the lost bank-notes!

Placing them in the fire, I watched the flames consume them, and from that night I commenced life afresh.

Jean is my secretary no longer. I effected a compromise with him, and at the present moment, owing to his shrewd business tact, combined with successful speculation, he is one of the most prosperous promoters of the South African mining companies in the City of London.

XI

DEATH-KISSES

The scene was composed of a bit of everything. An October evening, a dull sky, a fierce cold wind, and a woman. Yet the dreamy experience, where everything went at will, bears but little resemblance to reality.

The woman was sweet and tender; the interview passionate, yet innocent; and the words exchanged *naive* as the questions of a child.

The recollection of it leaves no poison of deception; only indelible remorse.

It was a chill, windy afternoon. In the morning a great thirst for fresh air had taken possession of me, and I joyfully left Brussels, counting on stopping at a little station I knew.

I think my journey terminated about four o'clock. Cutting across the fields, I entered a narrow path, paying but little attention to the way, and strolling aimlessly. I seemed to be in an incredibly careless and absent mood that day. I am not even certain that I got out at the right station, so drunk was I with the frenzy to communicate with nature.

Picture to yourself a rolling plain under a cheerless sky; with empty roads, cut in the brown earth, here and there made green with tender shoots; a few solitary and distant houses, and occasional stumps of leafless trees, red and melancholy-looking.

A flight of crows sailed slowly overhead, talking among themselves with little continuous croakings, flying always towards the setting sun. The day was grey, with deeper shades towards the horizon, stamping everything with a uniform tint. Children's voices sounded in the field. Suddenly three appeared, a boy and two girls, returning from school. They grew silent when they saw me, eyed me cautiously and crossed the path with quickened step. Soon I reached an isolated cross-road. A step further, and I encountered a strolling mountebank, with his wheeled home beside him. At my request he furnished me with a slight repast. Then, without saying a dozen words, I set off again, leaving the astonished man gaping at the money in his hand.

You say that I was mad.

Perhaps. At any rate, I was quite calm, but something evidently dominated and guided me. For of the three roads that spread out before me, why should I have chosen that one?

I assure you I have no spiritualistic tendencies, but there are times when I believe in a distinct influence.

The night had fallen, or rather, a sort of twilight, singularly lasting. A fine, cold rain, driven by a brisk wind, beat noisily upon my umbrella. I wandered slowly on. Holding it against the wind, I walked without effort. I think I must have slept, as I have only a vague recollection of that dreary promenade.

When I became aware of things around me, I was in front of a good fire. There was a dim consciousness of realising that the storm had redoubled its fury, that I had seen a light and knocked at a cottage door. As I recovered from the stupor, it seemed as if I had entered with some trivial formula of politeness; that I had seated myself in front of the genial flame as if I were in my own home.

A young woman, pale, but very beautiful, was sitting beside me. I glanced slowly around the room. We were alone. Little by little I remembered. It was she who had opened the door to me. Behold! even the card I gave her still in her hand. Were it not for her light breathing and the movement of her eyelids, I should say she was of wax.

She was older than myself, two or three years perhaps; tall and slight, with a gentle and melancholy grace. Her mouth, clear and tender, was near enough to the delicate nose to give her a slight appearance of a scolded child; the eyes were not large, but soft and pleading, and the oval of her face stretched the length of her blanched cheeks. Though sad, the face pleased me.

"How charming!" I exclaimed involuntarily, under my breath.

She must have heard the words, for she turned towards me and smiled.

"You are just as complimentary as of old—always the same Theophile."

In that voice I found an air of recognition. Instantly I remembered a half-forgotten period, like a pleasant dream; a name was upon my lips, but I could not utter it; I stammered a question.

"Well, well," she said. "They tell me I have altered, yet—why, don't you know Mariette?"

Mariette!

Mariette! only this thought, and I fell on my knees beside her; our hands touched, and I kissed her dainty white fingers. Why was I certain in all my life never to know a like moment?

Ah! never shall I experience the same mad joy; the delight of holding in mine the thin hands of my childhood's friend. It was that childhood I embraced; that other time, so free and pure, with its pretty welcoming air.

"Do you remember when last we met?" I asked earnestly.

She heaved a slight sigh, so like those of other days that tears rose to my eyes.

"Yes," she murmured. "But—there, don't speak of it. Such memories must be painful to both of us."

"If to you, none the less to me, Mariette," I replied, looking in her sad, sweet face.

Her lips quivered, and a tear stole down her cheek.

During a whole hour it was nothing but expressions of surprise and vain regrets. To the depths of our being we felt the force of these recollections, causing us to live over an almost forgotten period.

I found in looking at her, in listening to her, my great soul and little body of that sweet other time.

Once more I felt the immensity of the fields and of the sky; the fine smell of the leaves enthralled my senses, and the least sound was melody. Once more I lived the old free life over again. It was before I went to stay at Brussels, when I resided under the paternal roof on the edge of the dense Soignes forest, that Mariette and I were playmates and afterwards lovers.

How well I recollect one halcyon day, the memory of which now comes before me in all its vividness. It was autumn. We were walking alone in the wood. The leaves floated down noiselessly upon the chill November air, leaving the naked branches like black lace against a grey, snow-laden sky. That day she admitted that she loved me, that she would be my wife.

And all around us there was infinite space, coloured by the joyful imaginings of happy youth.

We were speaking of it, when suddenly she withdrew her hand from mine, and a red flush mounted to her forehead.

"But you soon forgot me when you went away," she said reproachfully. "I waited months, but you never wrote; then I heard how an actress had infatuated you. Yet—you are rich now, and the world looks leniently upon what it calls a wealthy man's folly."

I could not prevent myself from frowning.

"You mean Clementine Sucaret? People coupled our names without cause," I replied coldly, almost cruelly. Yet I knew she spoke the truth.

"And I—I am mad," she whispered.

I rose and looked at her. She was still seated, her eyes riveted upon the fire, her cheek resting upon her hand, appearing to have forgotten my presence. For a moment I remained in that position, then I reseated myself. There was nothing awkward in our silence. We felt too deeply for idle words. As we contemplated our past, the wind whistled without, the rain fell furiously, and from time to time I added a log to the fire and stirred the embers.

"Theophile," she exclaimed suddenly, looking me straight in the face, "it is your fault that I am married."

"Married?" I gasped in amazement. "I—I thought this cottage was your aunt's; that you kept house for her?"

There was a silence. The voice made me tremble, gay, careless idler that I was. She spoke slowly, without moving, as though giving utterance to the thought that possessed her. "When a woman is forsaken by the man she loves, who can blame her for a hasty, loveless marriage?" she asked. "You wrecked my life, Theophile, but I forgive you freely. After you had left, I was stricken down with grief, madness followed, and I accepted the first man who proposed to me. I did not love him; I—I shall never love him. And how could I? He is a dissolute ne'er-do-well, who spends his days in the *estaminet*, drinking cognac. It is I who am compelled to toil and earn money for him to spend in drink. Ah, Theophile, you little know how dull and utterly hopeless is my life!"

"But your husband, does he not try and make you happy?" I asked.

"Happy?" she cried, jumping to her feet and impetuously tearing open the bodice of her dress. "See! See, here; the marks of his violence, where he tried to murder me!" And she disclosed to my view her delicate breast disfigured by an ugly knife-wound, only partially healed.

"Horrible!" I exclaimed, with an involuntary shudder.

"That is not all," she continued, turning up her sleeves and revealing cruel bruises and lacerations upon her alabaster-like arms. "He wants to rid himself of me, to be free again; and when the brandy takes effect, he threatens to kill me."

"Why stay and be brutally ill-used in this manner?" I asked.

Shrugging her shoulders, she smiled sadly, replying, "If I were dead, it would end my misery. Should he ever know that you have been here, his jealousy would be so aroused that I believe he would carry his threat into effect."

"Come, come, Mariette, you must not talk like that," I exclaimed. "It grieves me to know of your unhappiness, to think that I am to blame."

"Remember, I forgive you."

"Yes, but try to bear up against it; do your duty to your husband, and thus compel him to treat you kindly."

"I have tried to do so, Heaven knows," she replied hoarsely, bursting into tears; "But everything is useless. Only death can release me."

"Don't talk so gloomily," I urged, taking one of her cold hands in mine. "Although we can be naught to one another save friends, let me be yours. I am ready to do anything you command me."

"You are kind, Theophile, very kind," she replied bitterly, shaking her head; "but friendship is poor reparation for love."

I thought of the years we had passed together at the time when years are so long and beautiful.

Finally I said to her—

"Tell me, what can I do for you?"

She made no answer, only her face appeared to grow a shade paler. With her eyes on the clock, she seemed to listen. "Nothing," she replied at last. "You—you must go."

"So soon?"

"Yes," she said, with a choking sob. "You ought not to have come here, and—and you must forgive me, Theophile, we women are so weak when memories are painful."

She wished to aid me in my preparations for departure, handed me my hat and buttoned my coat. We said nothing, but she lingered over the buttoning as though it were something very difficult.

Suddenly, with a bitter burst of tears, she flung her head down against my arm. She seemed such a frail little creature as I held her tightly and stroked away the tendril curls that strayed across her face.

I longed to console her, but could not give utterance to my thoughts.

"Mariette. Poor little Mariette," was all I could say.

"Good-bye, Theophile, good-bye," she whispered brokenly. "A great gulf separates us; you have gaiety and happiness, I only misery and despair. My husband—"

Just as suddenly as they commenced, her tears ceased. Clasping her hands, she lifted her agitated face to mine.

"Promise me—promise you will never return here again!"

I did not reply.

Bending over, her lips met mine in one fierce passionate caress.

Next second we were startled by a strange noise, sounding suspiciously like a footstep upon the gravel. We listened, but the sound was not repeated.

"Hark!" she whispered anxiously. "If my husband should find you here, would it not compromise me?"

With a force I should never have suspected, she led me to the door, and, after giving me a gentle push, locked it behind me.

"Adieu!" I murmured, as tenderly as I could.

There was no answer.

Through the keyhole I could see Mariette kneeling before a crucifix on the opposite wall.

Then I turned and went forth into the darkness.

THE MORNING WAS GREY AND dispiriting; the chill wind whirled the dead leaves in my path, and moaned through the bare branches as I walked up to the door of the cottage. My mind was perturbed by thoughts of what happiness might have resulted had I been true to the woman who loved me. I had spent a restless night at a roadside inn. Her misery tortured me, and, despite her entreaty, I was now on my way to again proffer assistance.

With trepidation I approached the door of the humble abode and knocked.

No one stirred. Everything seemed strangely silent.

About to repeat the summons, I noticed the door was ajar. Pushing it slowly open, I entered, at the same time uttering her name.

As I stepped into the neat, well-kept room, I at first saw nothing, but on glancing round the opposite side of the table, my eyes encountered a terrible sight.

Stretched upon the floor, Mariette was lying partly dressed, the pale light falling upon her upturned features. The cheeks and lips were bloodless; the eyes, wide-open, were staring wildly into space with a look of indescribable horror.

Falling upon my knees, I touched her face with my hand.

It was cold as marble. *She was dead*!

In her white breast a knife was buried up to the hilt, and from the cruel wound the blood had oozed.

She had been murdered!

The recollection of the events immediately following this ghastly discovery is but faint. I have a hazy belief that my mind became temporarily unhinged, that I left the place without informing any one of the tragedy; then, walking many miles through the forest, I reached a railway station, whence I returned to Brussels.

The one thing most in my mind was the terrible look of blank despair in the glazed eyes. I have never forgotten it. I shall carry its remembrance with me to the grave.

That awful look of reproach has ever since been uppermost in my memory. Try how I will, I cannot rid myself of its hideous presence.

A BRIGHT, CRISP MORNING IN December.

Hurrying down the Montagne de la Cour, where I chanced to have business, I came face to face with Clementine Sucaret, who, warmly clad in furs, was enjoying that harmless pastime so dear to the feminine heart—inspecting shop windows.

We had bid each other farewell three years before. She then left Brussels to fulfil engagements as a dancer in London and Paris, and since I heard nothing of her.

Greeting me with the same winsome smile and merry manner as of old, she inquired whither I was going. When I explained that my business was important, and did not admit of delay, she requested that she might accompany me, at the same time inviting me to *dejeuner* with her afterwards, an arrangement to which I consented without reluctance.

As we walked together, she commenced describing her adventures and successes, declaring that, after all, it was pleasant to return among old friends and cherished recollections. I was well aware at what she hinted when she said this, for I was one of her oldest friends, and had known her when she was only a *figurante* at the Theatre de la Monnaie, and lived with her decrepit and bibulous old father, a *concierge*, in the Rue du Trone. It was then that her cheerful, good-natured disposition and handsome face had fascinated me, causing me to forsake Mariette.

The thought inflicted a sharp twinge of remorse, for the tragedy in the little cottage was still fresh in my memory.

Having left her for a moment while I made a call, I rejoined her. Laughing and chattering, she chaffingly alluded to our former attachment, and pouted in feigned displeasure at what she termed my inconstancy.

Down the Rue de la Regence we had sauntered slowly, and were passing the imposing facade of the Palais de Justice, when suddenly she stopped, and, uttering an exclamation of surprise at the proportions of the vast building which had been completed in her absence, requested me to take her to see the interior.

Mounting the broad flight of granite steps, we passed into the magnificent marble hall.

Strange how Fate is constantly our mistress and rules our every action.

We had crossed under the gilded dome and were about to enter one of the court-rooms, when my eye caught a large printed notice fixed to the wall.

I halted and read.

It was an imposing poster, headed in great black capitals, "Court of Assize," and was the public announcement that Henri Pirlot had been sentenced to death by that tribunal for the wilful murder of his wife, Mariette, at a cottage near Spoel. It further stated that the condemned man had confessed that the cause of the crime was jealousy. He was intoxicated, and having discovered his wife kissing a strange man who had visited her in his absence, he went in and deliberately stabbed her to the heart!

"What a pair of idiots!" exclaimed Clementine, with a light laugh, as she read the notice. "The idea of killing a woman because she kissed her lover! Again, what a simpleton the woman was not to have been more wary! But—why—what's the matter, Theophile? You stand there gazing and looking as scared as if you'd seen a ghost. Any one would think *you* knew the rustic beauty, and were the strange lover!"

I started. A sickening sensation crept over me. The actress had little idea it was the terrible truth she uttered. I pleaded that I was not feeling well, and we left the building.

XII

The City in the Sky

In the mystic haze of the slowly dying day, a solitary Arab, mounted on a *meheri*, or swift camel, and carrying his long rifle high above his head, rode speedily over the great silent wilderness of treacherous, ever-shifting sand. Once he drew rein, listening attentively, and turning his keen dark eyes to the left, where the distant serrated crests of the mountains of Nanagamma loomed forth like giant shadows; but as nothing broke the appalling stillness, he sped forward again until at length he came to a small oasis, where, under a clump of palms, he made his camel kneel, and then dismounted.

As he stalked towards the lonely shrine of Sidi Okbar—a small domed building constructed of sun-dried mud, under which reposed the remains of one of the most venerated of Arab marabouts—he looked a young and muscular son of the Desert, whose merry bronzed face bore an expression of genial good-nature that was unmistakable, notwithstanding the fact that he belonged to the fiercest race of Bedouins. Tall and erect, he strode with an almost regal gait, even though his burnouse was brown, ragged, and travel-stained; the haick that surrounded his face was torn and soiled, and upon his bare feet were rough, heavy slippers, that were sadly the worse for wear. The latter, however, he kicked off on approaching the shrine, then, kneeling close to the sun-blanched wall, he cast sand upon himself, kissed the earth, and, drawing his palms down his face, repeated the Testification. In fervent supplication he bowed repeatedly, and, raising his voice until it sounded distinct on the still air, invoked the blessing of Allah. "O Merciful! O Beneficent Granter of Requests!" he cried; "O King of the Day of Faith, guide us, ere to-morrows sun hath run its course, into the path that is straight, and leadeth unto the *kasbah* of our enemies of Abea. Strengthen our arms, lead us in times of darkness and in the hours of day, destroy our enemies, and let them writhe in Al-Hawiyat, the place prepared for infidels, where their meat shall be venomous serpents, and they shall slake their thirst with boiling pitch."

Startled suddenly by a strange sound, he listened with bated breath. The thought occurred to him that his words might have been overheard by some spy, and instinctively his hand drew from his belt his *jambiyah*, the long, crooked dagger, that he always carried. Again a noise like a deep-drawn sigh broke the silence, and Hatita—for such was the young Arab's name—sprang to his feet and rushed round to the opposite side of the building, just in time to see a fluttering white robe disappearing in the gloom. With the agility of a leopard, the man of the Kanouri—the most daring of the slave-trading tribes in the Great Sahara—sprang towards it, and in twenty paces had overtaken the eavesdropper, who, with a slight scream, fell to earth beneath his heavy hand.

"Rise!" he cried, roughly dragging the figure to its feet, "thou son of Eblis!"

Next second, however, he discovered that the fugitive was a woman, veiled, enshrouded in her haick, and wearing those baggy white trousers that render all Arab females hideous when out of doors.

"Thou hast overheard my orison!" he cried, raising his knife. "Speak! speak! or of a verity will I strike!"

But the mysterious woman uttered no word, and Hatita, in a frenzy of desperation, tore the veil from her face.

Aghast he stood, and the knife fell from his fingers. The countenance revealed was amazingly beautiful, so charming, indeed, that instantly he became entranced by its loveliness, and stood speechless and abashed.

She was not more than eighteen, and her features, fair as an Englishwoman's, were regular, with a pair of brilliant dark eyes set well apart under brows blackened by kohl, and a forehead half hidden by strings of golden sequins that tinkled musically each time she moved. Upon her head was set jauntily a little scarlet *chachia*, trimmed heavily with seed-pearls, while her neck was encircled by strings of roughly-cut jacinths and turquoises, and in the folds of her silken haick there clung the subtle perfumes of the harem.

Slowly she lifted her fine eyes, still wet with tears, to his, and, with her breast rising and falling quickly, trembled before him, fearing his wrath.

"Loosen thy tongue's strings?" he cried at last, grasping her slim white wrist with his rough, hard hand. "Thou art from Afo, the City in the Sky, and thou hast gained knowledge of our intended attack?"

"Thy lips, O stranger, speak the truth," she faltered.

"Why art thou here, and alone, so far from thine home on the crest of yonder peak?" he inquired, gazing at her in wonderment.

"I came hither for the same purpose as thyself," she answered seriously, looking straight into his face—"to crave Allah's blessing."

"Art thou a dweller in the house of grief?" he asked. "Tell me why thou didst venture here alone."

She hesitated, toying nervously with the jewelled perfume-bottle suspended at her breast; then she answered, "I—I am betrothed to a man I hate. The Merciful Giver of Blessings alone can rescue me from a fate that is worse than death—a marriage without love."

"And who is forcing thee into this hateful union? If it is thy father, tell me his name."

"Yes, it is my father. His name is Abd el Jelil ben Sef e'Nasr, Sultan of Abea."

"The Sultan?" he cried in amazement. "Then thou art Kheira!" he added, for the extraordinary beauty of the only daughter of the Sultan of Abea was proverbial throughout the Great Desert, from Lake Tsad to the Atlas.

"Yes," she replied. "And from thy speech and dress I know thou art of the Kanouri, our deadliest enemies."

"True," answered the desert pirate. "To-morrow my tribe, to the number of ten thousand, now lying concealed in the valley called Deforou, will swarm upon thine impregnable city and—"

"Ten thousand?" she gasped, pale and agitated. "And thou wilt kill my father and reduce our people to slavery. Ah, no!" she added imploringly. "Save us, O stranger! Our fighting men went south one moon ago to collect the taxes at Dchagada, therefore we are unprotected. What can I do—how can I act to save my father?"

"Dost thou desire to save him, even though he would force upon thee this odious marriage?"

"I do," she cried. "I—I will save the City in the Sky at cost of mine own life."

"To whom art thou betrothed?" Hatita asked, tenderly taking her hand.

"To the Agha Hassan e Rawi, who dwelleth at Zougra, beyond the Nanagamma. He is three score years and ten, and 'tis said he treateth his wives with inhuman cruelty. One of his slaves told me so."

Hatita stood silent and thoughtful. Though he was a member of a tribe who existed wholly upon loot obtained from caravans and towns they attacked, yet so earnestly did the Sheikh's daughter appeal, that all thought of preserving the secret of the intended attack by murdering her disappeared, and he found himself deeply in love. His was a poor chance, however, he told himself. The proud Sultan of Abea would never consent to a brigand as a son-in-law, even if Kheira, known popularly as "the light of the eyes of the discerning," looked upon him with favour.

"To-night, O Daughter of the Sun, we meet as friends, to-morrow as enemies. Our spies have reported that thy city remaineth undefended, and, alas! there is a blood feud between my people and thine; therefore, when the hosts of the Kanouri enter with fire and sword, few, I fear, will be spared. Wilt thou not remain here with my tribesmen and escape?"

"No," she answered proudly. "I am a woman of Afo, and I will return unto my people, even though I fall before to-morrow's sundown under thy merciless swords."

As she spoke, one hand rested upon her supple hip, and with the other she pointed to the high shadowy peak whereon stood the great white stronghold known to the Arabs as the City in the Sky.

"But thou, who art like a sun among the stars, knowest our plans, and it is my duty to kill thee," he said, hitching his burnouse about his broad shoulders.

"I am in thine hands. If thou stainest them with my blood, thou wilt ever have upon thy conscience the remembrance that thou hast taken the life of one who was innocent of intrigue. If thou givest me freedom, I shall have at least one brief hour of felicity with my people before—before—"

And she sighed, without concluding the sentence.

"Thou, a fresh rose from the fountainhead of life, art in fear of a double fate, the downfall of to-morrow and the marriage feast next moon. Let not thy mind be troubled, for I stretch not forth the tongue to blame," he said at last, endeavouring to smile. "In Hatita, son of Ibrahim, thou hast a devoted friend, and one who may peradventure assist thee in a manner thou hast not dreamed. Therefore mount thine horse and return with all speed to Afo—not, however, before thou hast given me some little souvenir of this strange meeting."

"Thou slakest my thirst with the beverage of kindness!" she cried in joy. "I knew when first I saw thee that thou wert my friend."

"Friend?—nay, lover," he answered gallantly, as, taking her tiny hand again, he pressed her henna-stained nails softly to his lips. She blushed and tried to draw away, but he held her firmly until she withdrew one of her gold bangles from her wrist, and with a smile, placed it upon his.

"Behold!" she exclaimed, with a merry rippling laugh. "It is thy badge of servitude to me!"

"I am slave of the most handsome mistress in the world," he said happily. Then, urging her to warn the Sultan of the intentions of the Kanouri, he kissed her once tenderly upon the lips, lifted her into the saddle of her gaily caparisoned horse, and then she twisted her torn veil about her face, and, giving him "Peace," sped away swift as an arrow into the darkness, bearing intelligence that would cause the utmost sensation in the mountain fastness.

"I love her," murmured Hatita, when the sound of her horse's hoofs had died away. "But how can I save her? To-morrow, when we enter Afo and loot the Palace, she will be secured to grace our Sheikh's harem. No!" he cried, with a fierce, guttural imprecation. "She shall never fall into Nikale's brutal hands—never while I have breath!"

The sound of whispering caused him to fix his gaze upon a dark shadow thrown by some ethel-bushes, and next second, half a dozen men similarly attired to himself advanced.

"So, dog of a spy! thou hast betrayed us!" cried a voice, which in a moment he was startled to recognise as that of Mohammed El Sfaski, a kaid of his tribe.

"Yes," the others shouted with one accord; "We watched the son of offal speaking with the woman, and we overheard him telling her to warn the Sultan!"

"Follow her on the wings of haste!" cried the kaid. "Kill her, for death alone will place the seal of muteness upon the lips of such a jade;" and in a few seconds two white-robed figures vaulted into their saddles and tore past in the direction Kheira had disappeared.

"Speak!" thundered El Sfaski, who with the others had now surrounded him. "Knowest thou the punishment of traitors?"

"Yes," answered Hatita hoarsely.

"Who is the woman whose blackness and deceit hath captivated thee?"

Three rapid shots sounded in the distance. The Arabs had evidently overtaken and murdered the daughter of the Sultan! The young tribesman held his breath.

"I—I refuse to give thee answer," he said resolutely.

"By Allah! thou art a traitor to our lord Nikale, and of a verity thou hast also *A'inu-l Kamal*. Therefore shalt thou die!"

("The eye of perfection," or "evil eye," is considered by the Arabs to be so maleficent that it can not only injure, but kill a person.)

Then, turning to the others, he added—

"We have no time to bandy words with this accursed son of the Evil One. Tie him to yon tree, and let the vultures feast upon their carrion."

With loud imprecations the men seized their clansman, tore off his haick and burnouse, and bound him securely to a palm-trunk in such a position that he could only see the great expanse of barren sand. Then with that refinement of cruelty of which the nomadic Kanouri are past masters, they smeared his face, hands and feet with date-juice, to attract the ants and other insects; and, after jeering at him and condemning him to everlasting perdition and sempiternal culpability, they remounted their horses, and, laughing heartily, left him alone to await the end.

Through the long, silent night, Hatita, with arms and legs bound so tightly that he could not move them, remained wondering what terrible fate had befallen the beautiful girl who had overheard his orison. The two Arabs had not returned. He knew the men were splendid riders, therefore it was more than probable that they had very quickly overtaken her. Utterly hopeless, well knowing that to the blazing sun and the agonies of being half-devoured by insects he must very soon succumb, he waited, his ears on the alert to catch every sound.

In the sky a saffron streak showed on the edge of the sandy plain, heralding the sun's coming. He watched it gradually spread, knowing that each moment brought him nearer to an end of agony. He lifted his voice in supplication to Allah, and showered voluble curses upon the expedition about to be attempted by his tribe. The pale, handsome face of Kheira was ever before him, haunting him like a half-remembered dream, its beauty fascinating him, and even causing him to forget the horror of those hours of dawn.

Saffron changed to rose, and rose to gold, until the sun shone out, lighting up the trackless waste. The flies, awakened, began to torment the condemned man, who knew that the merciless rays beating down upon his uncovered head would quickly produce the dreaded delirium of madness. The furnace heat of sunshine grew intense as noon approached, and he was compelled to keep his eyes closed to avoid the blinding glare.

Suddenly a noise fell upon his ear. At first it sounded like a low distant rumbling, but soon his practised ears detected that it was the rattle of musketry and din of tom-toms.

The City in the Sky was being attacked! His tribesmen had arranged to deliver the assault at noon, but what puzzled him was a sullen booming at frequent intervals. It was the sound of cannon, and showed plainly that Afo was being defended!

From where he was he could see nothing of it. Indeed, the base of the mountain was eight miles distant, and the city, parched upon its summit, could only be approached from the opposite side by a path that was almost inaccessible. Yet hour after hour the rapid firing continued, and it was evident a most desperate battle was being fought. This puzzled him, for had not Kheira said that the city was totally undefended? Still, the tumult of battle served to prevent him from lapsing into unconsciousness; and not until the sun sank in a brilliant, blood-red blaze did the firing cease. Then all grew silent again. The hot poison-wind from the desert caused the feathery heads of the palms to wave like funeral plumes, and night crept on. The horrible torture of the insects, the action of the sun upon his brain, the hunger, the thirst, and the constant strain of the nerves, proved too much; and he slept, haunted by spectral horrors, and a constant dread of the inevitable—the half-consciousness precursory of death.

So passed the night until the sun reappeared, but Hatita's eyes opened not. The heat of the blazing noon caused him no concern, neither did the two great grey vultures that were hovering over him; for it was not until he heard voices in the vicinity that he gazed around.

One voice louder than the others was uttering thanks to Allah. He listened; then, summoning all his strength that remained, he cried aloud, in the name of the One Merciful, for assistance.

There were sounds of hurrying footsteps, voices raised in surprise, a woman's scream, and then objects, grotesquely distorted, whirled around him and he knew no more.

WHEN HATITA AGAIN OPENED HIS weary, fevered eyes, he was amazed to find himself lying upon a soft, silken divan in a magnificent apartment, with slaves watching, ready to minister to his wants. He took a cooling draught from a crystal goblet handed to him, then raised himself, and inquired where he was. The slaves made no reply, but, bowing low, left. Then in a few moments the *frou-frou* of silk startled him, and next second he leaped to his feet, and, with a cry of joy, clasped Kheira in his arms.

In her gorgeous harem dress of pale rose silk, with golden bejewelled girdle, she looked bewitching, though around her eyes were dark rings that betrayed the anxiety of the past few days. As their lips met in hot, passionate kisses, she was followed by a tall, stately, dark-bearded man of matchless bearing, whose robe was of amaranth silk, and who wore in his head-dress a magnificent diamond aigrette. Kheira saw him, and, withdrawing herself from Hatita's embrace, introduced her lover to her father, the Sultan of Abea.

"To thee I owe my life and my kingdom," said the potentate, giving him "Peace," and wringing his hand warmly. "Kheira hath related unto me the mercy thou didst show towards her; and it was thy word of warning that enabled us to repel and defeat the Kanouri."

"Then thou didst escape, O signet of the sphere of elegance!" the young Arab cried, turning to the Sultan's daughter.

"Yes; though I was hard pressed by two of thine horsemen I took the secret path, and thus were they baffled."

"The Director of Fate apprised our fighting men of their danger," said the Sultan; "and they returned on the same night. The breeze of grace blew, the sun of the favour of Allah shone. The news brought by Kheira was quickly acted upon, and the defences of the city so strengthened, that when at noon the assault was delivered, our cannon swept thy tribesmen from the pass like grains of sand before the sirocco. For six hours they fought; but their attempts to storm the city gate were futile, and the handful of survivors were compelled to retire, leaving nearly a thousand prisoners, including Nikale himself, in our hands."

"And how was I rescued?" Hatita asked, after briefly explaining how his conversation with Kheira had been overheard.

"On the day following the fight, we went unto the shrine of Sidi Okbar to return thanks to Allah, and there found thee dying of heat and thirst. Thou didst sacrifice thy life to save our ruler and his city, therefore we brought thee hither," she said.

"And as a reward," added the Sultan, smiling upon them both, "I give unto thee my daughter Kheira in marriage." Then, taking their hands, he placed them in each other's, and added, "Thou hast both the verdure of the meadows of life. May Allah preserve thee, and grant unto thee long years of perfect peace, and an eternal rose-garden of happiness. In order that thou shalt have position fitting the husband of thy Sultan's daughter, I have ordered our Palace of Kyoukoi to be prepared for thy reception. Therefore, wipe off the rust of ennui and fatigue from the speculum of thy mind, and follow me; for a feast is already prepared for the celebration of this betrothal."

And the happy pair, hand-in-hand, passed onward through the private pavilions—bewildering in their magnificence of marble and gold, and green with many leaves—to the Great Hall of the Divan, where, standing under the royal baldachin of yellow silk brocade, the Sultan of Abea rejoiced them with his favours, proclaiming Hatita, son of Ibrahim, as the future husband of Kheira, and appointing him Governor of the City in the Sky.

XIII

The Blood-Red Band

A series of exciting adventures that befell me four years ago were remarkable and puzzling. Until quite recently, I have regarded the mystery as impenetrable. Indeed, in this *fin-de-siecle* decade it is somewhat difficult to comprehend that such events could have occurred, or that the actors could have existed in real life.

I was in Piedmont, at the little village of Bardonnechia, a quaint, rural place comprising a few picturesque chalets, an inn, and a church with a bulgy spire, which nestles in the fertile valley at the foot of the towering, snow-capped Mont Cenis. I was staying at the inn, and I wished to go to Lanslebourg, on the opposite side of the mountain, intending to travel thence by diligence to Grenoble, where I had arranged to meet some friends. But I needed a guide. The by-paths in the Cottian Alps are rough and intricate, and he would be a daring spirit who would venture to cross the Cenis alone away from the beaten track.

There was not a single mule to be hired, and the only guide I could find refused to carry my valise, so I was in danger of missing my appointment. I could, of course, have gone by train through the tunnel to Modane, but that route would have taken me many miles out of my way, therefore I had decided upon the shorter road.

At evening, while I stood at dusk at the door of the inn, looking anxiously to see whether any guide or porter had returned from the mountains the innkeeper told me he had found a man.

"Does he come from the valley?" I asked.

"No, signore; from the mountains."

"Impossible? I should have seen him. I have been watching the path for an hour."

"This man does not follow the same path as the others."

"Why?"

But my host vouchsafed no further explanation; he only called with a loud voice, "Giovanni!"

The guide appeared. He was tall, muscular, and rather strange-looking, about thirty years old, the wrinkles of his face giving an expression of hard and energetic will. He had a large, straight nose, wide mouth, thick, bushy black hair, and a beard of several days' growth, while in his cap he wore a sprig of freshly-plucked edelweiss.

I invited him into my room, but he shrugged his shoulders.

"You wish to go to Lanslebourg, over the Cenis?" he said.

"Yes."

"Very well; give me ten lire."

The price was very moderate, but the fellow struck me as a swaggerer. Instinctively I did not like him.

"Where is your licence? Are you a regular guide?" I asked.

"I have no licence, but I have a certificate of honourable discharge. I was in the Fourth Regiment of Artillery."

"And your name?"

"Do you want to know all this for ten lire?" and he began to laugh sarcastically. "Very well; I will tell you my name gratis. I am called Giovanni Oldrini. Has the cross-examination concluded?"

Seeing that his smile displeased me, he immediately changed his expression, and added emphatically—

"Ask the landlord about me; he will tell you. *Buona sera*."

And he turned and left me abruptly.

At four o'clock next morning we set out. He tied my valise on his back, took his alpenstock, and set off nimbly, whistling a popular *chansonette*. His gait was peculiar. His step made no sound; he seemed to glide along.

Having crossed the rushing torrent by the ancient wooden bridge, we came to the foot of the mountain. Leaving the rough road that leads from Susa over the lower heights to Modane, we took a steep by-path that ran in serpentine wanderings over rocks and through woods of fir and pine. In climbing we passed a beautiful lavender garden. The side of the mountain was quite blue with the flowers, and the fresh air of dawn was scented by their fragrance. There were also barberries and gooseberries, and flowers which were among the first we know in our own land, such as dog-roses, white campions, and harebells. Then for some distance we skirted a wood, and as we went higher, the larches gave place to pines, and yet higher still only stunted herbage grew from the crevices of the bare brown rocks.

He climbed like a squirrel. Hardly had he started when he began to talk to me, but either from sleepiness or from the feeling of uneasiness which his company gave me, I did not answer him.

At first, in the steepest places, Giovanni turned and offered me his hand, but, being fresh, I refused his aid, proud to encounter the rough mountain. When we help ourselves with hands and knees, and every step must be studied, the mind does not notice the fatigue. Presently, however, the fellow began to walk by himself, abandoning me to my fate. There was no real danger, but I felt somewhat indignant at seeing him so high on the rocks.

Gradually he was increasing the distance between us, and I cried to him to stop, but my voice did not reach him. If it had not been for my valise, I would have returned immediately.

I saw he had a piece of paper in his hand and a pencil. Scribbling a few words, he folded the paper and placed it behind a large stone. My suspicions were increased when I saw him abstract something bright and shining from behind the stone and place it in his pocket. It was a revolver!

People do not generally go armed in the Cottian Alps, and I somehow felt convinced that the weapon was to be used for no lawful purpose. Perhaps the letter he had written was a message to his confederates, reporting the fact that he had secured a victim! How I regretted that I had not placed my revolver in my pocket instead of putting it in the valise he was carrying.

He was standing with his hands in his pockets, whistling a gay air and awaiting me. I was toiling up the steep path, and felt almost dead beat. The whole mountain was a mass of gigantic rocks, half buried in the sand, soft and moist from recently melted snow and the draining of the ice.

"I was looking for a franc-piece I dropped. It rolled behind that stone, and I cannot find it," he said. Then he looked into my eyes, and asked, with an insolent air, "Don't you believe me?"

"No."

I did not believe him, and began to be greatly disquieted. He perceived it, and immediately became jovial and talkative. He knew me, he said—he had asked the innkeeper about me. He knew that I was a journalist; it must be a fine trade for making money by the sackful. He knew city life, for he had lived in Turin, and he always read the *Secolo*—it was his favourite paper. He also knew that I had written novels—another gold mine. Writers of romance, he supposed, were always seeking adventure, and poking their noses in out-of-the-way corners, and inquiring into other people's business. Good! I was with him, and might meet with a strange experience presently.

But I paid no attention to him.

"You gentlemen come to the Alps for the fun of knowing what fatigue is," he said. "Ah! if you only knew what it was—how much a piece of bread costs!"

He was eloquent and excitable, and spoke like a man believing himself to be followed by constant persecution.

We had almost reached the summit, when suddenly we came upon a rough pillar built of pieces of rock piled together.

"See!" he said; "there is the frontier mark."

Then we continued walking a dozen paces or so, and were in France.

Soon afterwards we recommenced our ascent to the summit, trudging through patches of melted snow. For about half an hour we continued our rough climb, when he halted, and, scanning the mountain cautiously, said—

"Come, follow me quickly!"

"Where?" I asked. "This surely is not the road to Lanslebourg?"

"Do not argue, but come with me," he said impatiently. "If you do not, it will be the worse for you!" he muttered between his teeth.

Linking his arm in mine, he half dragged me along to what appeared to be the face of a perpendicular rock. We passed along a narrow passage behind a great boulder, and as we did so, my strange guide gave a shrill whistle.

In a moment a cunningly-concealed door in the face of the rock opened and a wild-haired, black-bearded, brigandish-looking man emerged.

I was alarmed, for I saw I had been entrapped.

My guide uttered a few words in the Piedmontese *patois*, which I did not understand, whereupon the man who had opened the door exclaimed—

"The signore Inglese will please enter."

I hesitated, but I saw that to refuse was useless, so together we went into a large dark cavern. The bolt of the door was shot back into its socket with an ominous sound, while our footsteps echoed weirdly through the distant recesses. The man took up a torch and guided us through intricate turnings, until at last we came to a door which he opened, and we found ourselves in a small natural chamber, with wonderful stalactites hanging from the roof.

Two sinister-looking men, who were seated at a rough deal table drinking and playing dominoes, rose as we entered.

Neither spoke, but the man who had admitted us poured out some cognac and handed it to me, afterwards filling the other glasses. The men lifted them to me and tossed off the contents, an example which I followed.

"We are safe here," observed Giovanni, turning to me; "safe from the storm, the frontier guards, from everything."

"I engaged you to conduct me to Lanslebourg, not to bring me here," I said severely.

He smiled.

"This cave has been the grave of many men," he replied, as he calmly selected a cigar from the box upon the table. "It may be yours."

"What do you mean?" I cried, thoroughly alarmed.

"Surely you understand," exclaimed the man who admitted us. "We are outlaws, brigands, contrabandists—whatever you like to call us in your language—it is quite immaterial. Come with me and I will convince you."

Again I hesitated.

"Follow!" he commanded, taking up the torch.

Together we descended a short flight of roughly-hewn steps into a small, dark, damp-smelling cavern below. As he lifted the torch above his head, I saw that the place was occupied.

I shuddered and drew back in horror.

Upon a heap of dirty, mouldy straw, lay a woman. Her dress was ragged and faded, but she was very beautiful, with light golden hair, and a face that betokened culture and refinement. Around her neck was a curious band of a blood-red colour. Upon her countenance was a ghastly pallor, the lips were bloodless, the jaw had dropped, the eyes were fixed and had a stony, horror-stricken look in them, for she was a corpse!

"You are satisfied that we are brigands?" he asked. "Good! Now I will show you that we are contrabandists."

Ascending the steps, we went to another part of the great cave, where he showed me kegs of cognac and wine, boxes of cigars, silks, and an assortment of dutiable merchandise.

When we returned to where the other men were sitting, one of them, the elder of the party, who spoke with authority, addressed me.

"Well," he said, "you have seen our stronghold, and recognise the impossibility of any one escaping from here, eh?"

"Yes," I replied; "but I cannot conceive why I have been allured here. I am a poor man, and not worth robbing."

"That is not our intention, signore," the contrabandist answered, with mock politeness, as he puffed a cloud of smoke from his rank cigar. "True, you have been entrapped, but if you consent to perform for us a small secret service, you are at liberty to depart; and, moreover, our good Giovanni will complete his contract, and see you safely to Lanslebourg."

"What is the service?" I asked.

"It is not at all difficult, and you will run no risk," he replied. He took from an ancient oak coffer a small sealed packet, and added, "We desire this taken to Briancon; will you undertake to do so?"

"What am I to do with it?" I asked.

"The thing is simple enough. You will leave here and go to Lanslebourg, thence to Briancon. Arrived there, you will remain at the Couronne d'Or, and wear this peace of edelweiss in your coat. On the day after to-morrow, a lady will call upon you and ask for the packet, as promised. She will give her name as Madame Trois Etoiles, and will give you a receipt for the packet. This you will send to Giovanni Oldrini at the Poste Restante at Bardonnechia. There the matter will end."

"If she does not call?"

"Then you must advertise to find her, announcing that you particularly desire an interview. Of course your undertaking will be binding, and you will preserve the secret of the existence of this place under penalty of death. Do you agree?"

I glanced round the weird cavern. The last straw of my self-possession was broken, and I was prepared to promise anything in order to escape.

"Agree, signore," urged Giovanni anxiously. "There will be no risk, no inconvenience, I assure you."

"Very well," I said at last; "if you stipulate this as the price of my ransom, I suppose I am compelled to submit."

"You will swear to preserve our secret; to tell no living soul where you obtained the packet, and to deliver it without fail and with the seals intact?" the elder man asked, handing me a carved ivory crucifix.

"Yes, I swear," I said, taking it and pressing it to my lips.

"Good!" he exclaimed; "here is the packet. Deliver it safely, for its contents, if lost, could never be replaced. Join us in another glass, and then proceed. Oldrini will go with you to the outskirts of Lanslebourg."

I emptied another glass of brandy with the smugglers, and a few minutes later saw the sunlight and breathed the fresh mountain air again. When we were well on our downward path, I felt inclined to reprimand my guide for having taken me to the cavern; but on reflection it became plain that he was in league with the contrabandists, and that he carried on smuggling and thieving in the guise of guide.

Onward we trudged down the steep, slippery rocks, scarcely uttering a word for an hour, when suddenly from a sentry-box there appeared a French soldier with rifle presented.

He inquired our names, and why we wished to enter France. A civil reply propitiated him, and he drew himself up at "Attention!" and allowed us to proceed.

We were compelled by the steepness of the mountain to take a circuitous route, so that the descent occupied longer than we had anticipated, and when, soon after sunset, we emerged upon the high road to Lanslebourg, he halted to take leave of me.

"Pardon, signore," exclaimed my guide. "I only took you to the cavern because it is imperative that the packet should be delivered. I ask your forgiveness;" and he raised his cap deferentially.

"For what reason is it imperative?" I inquired.

"I regret I cannot tell you," he replied. "*Addio*, signore. Remember your trust, and keep your promise, or—"

He did not finish the sentence, but shrugged his shoulders significantly, and, handing me my valise, turned and left me.

Two DAYS LATER, I WAS sitting idly smoking at a little table outside the Couronne d'Or inn at Briancon, that curious little town inside the great fortress that commands the pass of Mont Genevre. The Alps were purple in the glorious sunset. The sun had long ago been hidden by the mountains behind, on whose tops the ice and snow glistened. Then, as the calm twilight came on, a pale, rosy light suffused the eastern sky, the moon rose, the aspens shook, the outlines of the valley shaded off into darkness and uncertainty, and the last glow sank into the deepening blue.

Having telegraphed to my friends, arranging to meet them at Grenoble on the morrow, I sat silent, thoughtful, and expectant.

Suddenly a musical voice behind exclaimed in English.

"The signore wears the edelweiss, I observe."

"Yes," I replied, turning and confronting a tall, handsome, middle-aged lady, attired in deep black. She was evidently of the upper class, and spoke English with an accent scarcely perceptible. A fact which struck me as very remarkable was that around her neck she wore a band of blood-red silk exactly the same as that upon the corpse in the brigand's cave! What could it denote?

"I presume I am not mistaken in addressing you. I am Madame Trois Etoiles."

"I have been expecting you," I said.

"You have been commissioned to deliver something to me, have you not?" she asked, seating herself in the chair on the opposite side of the table.

"Yes. I must confess, however, that my mission is a somewhat mysterious one." And I drew the packet from my pocket.

"Mine is also mysterious," she laughed nervously. "But tell me, who gave it to you?"

"Unfortunately, I must not tell, madame; I am sworn to secrecy," I replied. Then I asked, "Why is it imperative that the packet should be conveyed to you in this manner?"

"Ah, signore, I am as ignorant as yourself. Besides, I also have taken an oath. It was a stipulation that I should explain nothing. I was to meet you here and receive the packet—to act as messenger, in fact. That is all."

"Then we cannot exchange confidences," I said disappointedly.

She shook her head.

"Very well; there is the mysterious packet;" and I handed it to her.

Then I tore a leaf from my pocket-book, and, together with a pencil, handed it to my strange visitor, who wrote in Italian the words, "Received of Signore the Englishman, the packet with seals intact.— Madame * * *"

Passing the paper back to me, she drew on the glove she had removed, and, rising, wished me a haughty adieu, remarking that she was obliged to leave for Modane by the diligence which would start almost immediately from the Hotel de Ville.

I raised my hat, and after a graceful bow she turned, and, walking away along the quiet, old-world street, was soon lost in the gathering gloom.

ONE EVENING, QUITE RECENTLY, I was sitting in the Trattoria di Piazza San Carlo, that great, gilded restaurant that overlooks the handsome square in the centre of Turin. Major Malaspina, of the National Guard, was with me, and we were chatting over our coffee and cigars. Giulio Malaspina is an old friend whom I first met ten years ago, when, in the performance of my journalistic duties, I visited the cholera hospitals of Naples with King Humbert and Queen Margherita. Mainly through him, various facilities were afforded me for visiting the hospitals and passing the military *cordon* as often as I pleased, hence our acquaintance ripened into warm and lasting friendship. Short and thick-set, with closely-cropped, iron-grey hair, and a fierce, bristly moustache, he is a merry little man, and at the present time the most popular officer of the Turin garrison.

He was glancing through the *Tribuna*, which the waiter had just brought, while I sat lazily contemplating the groups of diners through a veil of tobacco smoke.

"Ah!" he exclaimed suddenly, removing the cigar from his lips and looking up from the paper. "I see they've captured a band of robbers in the Carpathians. It is really remarkable that brigands should exist in Europe in these highly civilised days."

"Are there any in the Alps?" I asked, half inclined to relate my extraordinary experience, but suddenly remembering that I had bound myself to secrecy.

"There were, but there are none now. I assisted in clearing out the last band. They were clever, daring scoundrels, who exhibited much remarkable ingenuity. The discovery of the gang caused a good deal of sensation about two years ago. But of course you were in England at that time; possibly you heard nothing about it?"

"No; tell me," I said anxiously. "I'm always interested in stories of brigands."

"Plots for novels, eh?" he said, laughing merrily, contemplating the fine diamond that glittered on his finger. "Well," he began, "for a long time it had been known that a number of contrabandists were smuggling goods from France over the almost impassable summit of Mont Cenis."

"They were Piedmontese brigands, then?" I exclaimed in surprise.

"Yes. Travellers had been robbed, diligences on the Modane road had been stopped, baggage rifled, and various depredations were being constantly reported. It was evident that they were in league with some receivers of stolen property at Milan, but the ingenious manner in which they disposed of their booty baffled all efforts to discover the identity of the thieves. Probably they would have continued their nefarious operations unmolested until the present time, had they not committed a most daring robbery, which very nearly culminated in a public scandal. *Per Bacco*! there is more comedy than tragedy in the story. You must be discreet if I relate it to you, for it is not generally known, and if it got about, a good deal of displeasure might be created at the Ministry at Rome."

And, amused at his own thoughts, he laughed heartily.

"It happened about three years ago," he continued, "that the King, while inspecting the crown jewels, discovered that the small jewelled cross which surmounts the great historic diamond of enormous value that forms the apex of the royal crown was loose, and, moreover, the great gem itself required resetting. After much consideration, it was at length resolved to entrust the work to a renowned jeweller in Paris, and the portion of the insignia was dispatched thither by royal messenger. The latter, it appears, took train by way of Turin and the Mont Cenis tunnel, but on arrival at the Alpine frontier, found that some repairs were being carried out in the tunnel, which necessitated it being closed to all traffic for several days. He was unable to walk through, because there had been a landslip. That the crown should be renovated without delay was imperative, as it was required for an important State ceremonial, therefore the messenger resolved to go by mule over the mountain to Modane. On the way, however, he and his guide were attacked, and the contrabandists carried away, among other things, the precious packet containing the most valuable portion of the regal crown!"

The major's eyes twinkled merrily, and he laughed immoderately. Suddenly, noticing my grave, anxious expression, he said—

"Ah, of course you are interested! *Dio mio*! it was a huge joke. You desire to hear the *denouement*? Well, you may easily imagine His Majesty's wrath when the matter was reported to him; but the gravity of the situation lay in the fact that any hue and cry raised would create a public scandal, and in all probability cause the thieves to destroy the jewels. Had the newspapers got wind of the theft, the whole of Europe would be laughing at Italy's ludicrous discomfiture. For several weeks the frontier guards kept a sharp look-out on the mountains, but no traces of the thieves could be discovered, therefore at Rome a good deal of anxiety began to be felt. At length, however, the King himself received a letter from the scoundrels, stating that they had discovered the nature of their booty, and as loyal subjects of His Majesty, and upholders of the dignity of the kingdom, they desired to return the portion of the crown. They stipulated, however, that the packet containing the jewels would only be given up to the Countess di Palermo, one of the queen's ladies-in-waiting, and that if she called on a certain evening at an inn at Briancon, the packet would be duly delivered to her. Cool, audacious impudence, wasn't it?"

"Yes," I said; "but how ineffably loyal they were!"

"Most extraordinary rascals! Of course the King gave a pledge that no attempt would be made to trace whence the jewels came, and that the Countess alone would keep the appointment. She did so; and, remarkable to relate, the packet was handed to her by some wayfaring Englishman, whose name never transpired. In that manner the most valuable of the crown jewels was recovered, greatly to the satisfaction of His Majesty, the Council of Ministers, and all who were in the secret."

Malaspina puffed vigorously at his cigar for a few seconds, and then continued—

"The recklessness of the outlaws was amazing. Robbery and extortion became more frequent, and thefts were committed with as cool determination as if the scoundrels held special licence from the King. At length the Minister of Police decided that such a state of things should no longer be allowed to continue. Hence it was that I found myself at the head of a company of Bersaglieri, scouring the mountains from Mont Blanc to Mont Rosa. After much fruitless search, we discovered that the stronghold of the bandits was a remarkable cave almost on the summit of the Cenis, at a point accessible only by a secret by-path. Having carefully laid our plans, we advanced to the attack early one morning. Unfortunately, the mountain afforded no cover, therefore our presence must have been immediately detected. Eventually, however, we battered down the door of their hiding-place, and entered. To our surprise, we found the cavern was an enormous one, and it took us a considerable time to explore its recesses. In the meantime, the occupants, whoever they were, must have escaped by another exit, for we never saw them, and they have not been apprehended to this day. In the cavern I found quantities of contraband goods stored, and every evidence of extensive smuggling. One discovery I made was indeed horrible, yet on closer investigation it proved as grimly humorous as the other incidents. Into a lower chamber I had descended with a light, and found, to my amazement, the body of a beautiful woman, who had evidently been kept a prisoner, and had died under harsh treatment. Apparently she had expired quite recently, for there were no signs of decomposition. At first I felt inclined to retreat, but the expression in the wide-open, staring eyes attracted my attention, and I bent and touched the face. It was clammy and cold, but quite hard. A portion of it came off in my hand. *Dio*! I had been deceived—it was of wax!"

"Wax?" I cried, astonished.

"Yes. Inquiries I subsequently made showed that a travelling waxwork show on its way across the frontier had been attacked a couple of years before, and among other things stolen was this wax figure. With cunning ingenuity, the contrabandists had contrived to transform the ruddy visage of a wax 'Desdemona' into the pallid countenance of a corpse, which they placed upon a heap of filthy straw in the damp, dark lower chamber. Around its neck, for some reason unaccountable, they had placed a scarlet band, similar to that always worn by the Countess di Palermo to conceal a cicatrice. The object, I suppose, was to show the corpse to travellers, whom they entrapped in order to extort money from them by threatening to keep them in the Dantean dungeon, and starving them to death."

"A most ingenious device," I said in abject astonishment. "The cave is now deserted, I suppose?"

"The cave? *Pouf*!" and he raised both his hands with a movement indicative of an explosion. "Acting under orders from Rome, a party of engineers blew it up with dynamite. As regards the thieves, no one knows what became of them. It must be admitted, however, that they had one redeeming characteristic—that of loyalty to their exemplary sovereign!"

And Major Malaspina laughed, sipped his vermouth, and lapsed into the full enjoyment of his long cigar.

XIV

A Child of the Sun

S adness and joy, despair and ecstasy, were never so linked as they are in my soul to-night.

Many men have gone mad upon far less provocation, and yet I am calm—so calm with this whirligig of emotions that I surprise myself.

Ah! it will not be long ere it is all over. Death will bring oblivion, the game will stop; and though joy, ecstasy, and delight all flee, sadness, misery, and despair will be banished with them. Remorse will cease to gnaw—that everlasting longing for what can never be will end its torture, and I shall be at peace.

But if there should not be rest beyond the grave? Bah! I'm upset, and I imagined I was calm. There is a superlative in suffering as in everything, else, and I have reached it. Death at its worst can have no further horrors.

Three drops from this phial in my hand into that glass of cognac at my elbow, and my ticket is made out. One gulp, and I shall have started on my journey.

Ah! it was not an unpleasant draught—slightly bitter, perhaps. The spirit was strong—a bitter potion, a sweet release.

It is merely a question of time; a few minutes now, and I shall be carried from the here to the hereafter.

How strangely my memory stirs! Am I dreaming? Or am I really growing young again?

It is the evening of a hot August day. The sun has disappeared in a blaze of crimson and gold. The breeze rises, and the broad. Plage at Scheveningen is swept by the refreshing wind scudding across the North Sea. Long, sharp-crested, snowy waves are breaking into hissing spray on the shore, and, chased in by the heavy weather, the picturesque Dutch fishing-smacks fly like gulls to reach the anchorage behind the lighthouse towards Loosduinen.

The Casino is ablaze with light on top of the high dune dominating the villas and hotels that line the beach. There is dancing this evening, for the season is "at its height," as *Le Petit Courrier* says.

Men of the *haut ton* are promenading on the broad terrace, and gazing on the file of fair ladies who are arriving, one after the other, in ball dress. They are mainly Belgians in queer hats, and Parisians in limp cravats, but there are some Dutch and English among them, and these are none the less merry.

Close to me half a dozen loungers are smoking cigars and talking loud enough for me to overhear. A handsome, elderly fop sets the key, and the others laugh in chorus whenever he utters a *bon mot*.

"I'm open to bet that the lovely Valerie de Noirville will not come," he says. "Her foster-father has left her to mope alone at the Deutschmann. He is already sitting at the ecarte-table, where he stands alone against all comers. I'm afraid, my dear Victor, you'll not see your incomparable Valerie this evening."

"I confess that, after all, I don't care very much," replies the person addressed, shrugging his shoulders. "This Southron is too dark-skinned, and has got a hasty temper too. For me, I only like the blondes."

"That may be, but her millions will please you, I fancy. It is an open secret that mademoiselle is the favourite in the will, and she certainly is a most fascinating girl."

"De Noirville hasn't the least desire to have his will executed just yet. Besides, why should I waste time over her? The place is taken already."

"At Paris, yes—by Rene Delbet; everybody knows that—but at Scheveningen—?"

"The same here, the same here, old fellow. The lady with the black eyes never pines alone—not even at seaside resorts. What is amusing, is that our excellent friend, De Noirville, does not notice how desperately his daughter flirts. Yet he's seen a great deal of life, and if I had been married twice, I think I should know how to play the watch-dog."

"Eh? Has she a cavalier here? Who—who?"

"A poor devil of a lieutenant in the Chasseurs d'Afrique. He adores her, and believes he has no rival. Nobody knows him; he is a mere chance-met gallant."

"Infernal impertinence, to aspire to the hand of *la belle* Valerie!" remarks one.

"Is it a serious affair?" inquires another.

"Was Valerie ever serious?" asks the elder man, with a laugh. "No, my dear fellows, she's only serious with Rene Delbet; but then, he's one of the richest men on the Bourse."

I turn away to hide myself, for they are speaking of me. I, Lucien Peyrafitte, am the "poor devil of a lieutenant," and it is true that I adore Valerie, the charming girl of whom those jays had spoken with so much recklessness. Although I had known her for several months,—first in Paris, and afterwards here, on the Dutch coast,—I had not breathed one word of love.

Why should I not do so to-night? She was alone at the hotel; there could be no more fitting opportunity.

Retracing my steps along the Plage to the Hotel Deutschmann, I found her sitting upon the verandah alone, plunged in a deep reverie. In one of those huge wicker chairs which one sees nowhere else but at Scheveningen, I took a seat beside her, and, grasping her white hand, raised it to my lips.

How long I sat there I cannot tell. It must have been several hours. Before we rose to enter the hotel, she had admitted that she loved me, and as a pledge of her affection, had given me a turquoise ring from her finger, while I had kissed her passionately, she returning my caresses and appearing supremely happy.

Yet it was in a brief fool's paradise that I existed that night, for before midday on the morrow I had left Scheveningen, having received a telegram from one of my comrades in Paris, urging me to return at once, as the regiment was ordered to Africa immediately.

Such was the irony of fate! Just as I had won the love of the woman I worshipped, I was torn away from her without scarcely an opportunity of bidding her farewell.

"WE MAY ALL THREE DIE to-night!"

The words were spoken by Captain Lavigniac, who with myself and Lieutenant Maurel were crouching around the dying embers of our camp-fire.

"That's true," remarked Maurel; "but if so, we shall die for France. And, after all, is life worth living?"

We laughed, *blasé boulevardiers* that we were. Having been nauseated by the sweets of life, we were now face to face with death.

The expedition against the fanatical Kel-Ahamellen was much more perilous than we had anticipated. General La Pelletier, who commanded the Algerian forces, had sent us—a mere handful of men— from In Salah away into the wild, inhospitable Tanezrouft Desert, in pursuit of a horde of the dusky rebels; but the long weary ride across the burning plains to Djedeyyed had taken all the spirit out of us. Under a blazing sun we had been journeying for a week, and on this particular night were encamped in a small oasis of Am Ohannan, which consisted of a well of brackish water and one single palm.

Unfortunately, owing to the treachery of our native guide,—who, by the way, was summarily dealt with by being shot,—we had entered a trap laid for us by the enemy. Our scouts had only an hour before reported that we were surrounded by the Arabs, who greatly outnumbered us, and that our position was extremely grave.

We were, therefore, waiting in the momentary expectation of a night attack.

For myself I did not care. Since my arrival in Africa I had received several warm, affectionate letters from Valerie; but, alas! my awakening had come. By the same mail that had brought her last letter to Algiers, I had received from a friend a *Figaro*, which contained the following announcement in its "High Life" column:—

> "A marriage has been arranged, and will shortly take place between Mademoiselle Valerie de Noirville, who is well-known in Paris society, and Monsieur Rene Delbet."

Perfidious fate! I had been tricked by her, and all her declarations of love were false. Heartsick and jaded, I sat beside the smouldering embers, thinking over the hopelessness of my future. The discovery of Valerie's baseness had crushed me. With the exception of the crackling of the fire, and the measured tread of the sentry beyond, all was still in the bright, clear night. Around the well our men were lying, wrapped in their cloaks, but not sleeping. Each man, with his revolver in one hand and the bridle of his horse in the other, was ready at any moment to spring up, mount, and ride straight into the irregular column of brown-faced, white-burnoused foe, who had sworn on their Koran to exterminate us Christian dogs.

The moments passed, breathless and exciting.

"*Qui est la?*" suddenly demanded a sentry, causing us to start.

"*Ami. Pour la France!*" was the response, and in a moment later Colonel Chadoume joined us.

"There will be fighting to-night," he said briefly. "There are thousands of those black devils."

"There will not be so many when our sabres have whirled through them," observed Lavigniac grimly.

"We are caught like rats in a trap," whispered the colonel in a low tone, so that the men should not overhear his misgivings. "The only way in which we can save ourselves is to apprise Le Pelletier of our position, and give him a plan of the country between In Zize and Chikh Salah from the survey we have made."

"But how can we?" asked Maurel. "Whoever went would have to pass the lines of the enemy at the risk of being shot."

We were silent for several minutes.

"I will go," I said at last.

"You?" exclaimed the three men in surprise.

I nodded.

"I will make the attempt," I added.

"But you must carry the plan as well as the letter, and start before daybreak," said the colonel.

"I am ready," I replied. I set but little value upon my life, for, truth to tell, I was utterly reckless now Valerie was false to me.

In the grey hour before the dawn I left the camp. I had exchanged my scarlet trousers and gilt-braided tunic for a shapeless white burnouse, and about my head wore a haick, around which was twisted many yards of brown camel's hair; my face had been effectually dyed a deep brown, I had assumed a flowing black beard, and my bare feet were thrust into rough slippers. Any one who had met the inoffensive Arab trader from El Biodh, would scarcely have suspected him to be an officer of the Chasseurs d'Afrique, and a well-known figure in drawing-rooms of the Avenue de Champs Elysees.

Mounted on a camel, with well-filled bags across my saddle, I rode slowly along, over the rough stony desert, eastward, guided only by the streak of yellow light that heralded the dawn.

Far away upon the horizon was a low range of hills, at the foot of which the Kel-Ahamellen were encamped.

I knew it was useless to evade passing through their lines by taking a circuitous route, and had decided that it would be safer to act boldly, and endeavour to pass through their headquarters.

For hours I rode wearily onward. The pitiless rays of the blazing sun beat down upon the loose, parched earth, and their reflection almost blinded me. Not a breath of wind cooled the atmosphere, but, on the contrary, the blasts which ever and anon blew over the Great Sahara, whirling up dense clouds of sand, were like whiffs of hot air from a furnace.

The sun travelled its course, and sank behind me with a blood-red, angry glare that bathed the desert and mountains with brilliant tints. By shading my eyes with my hands, I could now distinguish that I was approaching the settlement of the hostile tribe, and could make out their scattered tents.

As I looked, I saw four figures approaching. They grew nearer rapidly. Then I saw they were mounted Arabs, galloping with all speed towards me. They were standing in the stirrups in the manner peculiar to the Bedouins of the Great Desert, and, with their long rifles carried high above their heads and their white burnouses flowing behind, were bearing down upon me.

Drawing a long breath, I collected all the courage I possessed.

A few minutes later, with wild yells, the brown-visaged quartette rode up to me, addressing rapidly-uttered questions in Arabic, which I answered coolly.

I told them that I had no sympathy with war, that I was a trader from El Biodh, and that my destination was In Salah, where I constantly had commercial transactions.

"But how camest thou here?" asked the great black-bearded fellow who had first addressed me, as he fixed his keen eyes upon mine.

"I rode," I replied in Arabic, a language in which I was fortunately proficient. "Allah hath protected me."

"Didst thou not see the red-legged French dogs?"

"Yes, I passed them yesterday. There are thousands of them."

This statement seemed to cause them considerable dismay. They held a hurried conversation in an undertone, and then informed me that I should have to go before the Sheikh.

An hour later, I was taken before the chief of the tribe, who was seated cross-legged on a mat outside his tent. He was a grey-bearded, wizen-faced old man, whose eyes had lost none of the dark brilliance of youth, and whose teeth shone white in contrast with his red lips and sun-tanned yellow face. As I was led up to him, and the manner in which I had been discovered explained, he slowly removed his long pipe from his mouth, and regarded me critically.

"Thou sayest the French, the accursed offspring of Eblis, are numerous? Where didst thou see them?"

"In an oasis near Tighehert."

"Ah! thine accent! Thou speakest French, then?"

"Yes, father," I replied; "I learned it in Algiers."

He grunted dubiously, and, turning to a great brawny giant who stood among the followers who crowded around him leaning upon their guns, uttered a few guttural words.

"Did not the sons of offal stop thee?" he inquired. "Relate unto me all thou knowest about them."

"I know nothing," I replied, bowing submissively. "I merely passed, having satisfied them that I was not a spy. I had no object in interesting myself in the movements of infidels."

The old Sheikh replaced his chibouk between his lips and continued smoking in thoughtful silence, having fixed his gaze intently upon me.

"Hum!" he grunted.

Then he proceeded to interrogate me regarding my ride from El Biodh. My replies, however, did not apparently remove his suspicions, and he smiled sarcastically now and then, at the same time watching contemplatively the thin columns of blue smoke that rose from his pipe. Suddenly he turned, and, addressing the men who had ridden out to meet me, gave orders that I should be searched.

I stood silently by, watching the men turn out and examine closely the contents of my saddlebags, and the food I was carrying. Then they proceeded to search my pockets, compelling me to raise my arms above my head.

Peste! Fate was again unpropitious!

As I raised my hands, my loose burnouse fell from my arms, leaving them bare, and disclosing that they were white!

"Ah!" cried the Sheikh, his bright eyes flashing with anger. "So thou art a spy! Thou, son of a dog, seekest the overthrow of Allah's chosen!"

"My father," I cried, "I—I am not a spy. Behold! I have neither knife nor gun. Is it not written that the One Worthy of Praise showeth mercy only to the merciful?"

"Seize the dog! Take him away, and let him be shot at dawn, as soon as there is sufficient light to distinguish a black thread from a white," the old rebel commanded with a wave of his sun-tanned hand.

Then, rising, he cast aside his pipe impatiently, and was about to enter his tent, when his passage was barred by a veiled girl in rich silks and gauzes, who stood for a moment gazing at me. Her *adjar*, although concealing her face, left visible a fine pair of sparkling black eyes, and a forehead that had been plentifully bedaubed with powder in the manner of Eastern women. Rows of golden sequins hung upon her brow, and upon her wrists and bare ankles were jingling bangles.

"Hold!" she cried in a commanding tone, raising her bare arm and addressing the Sheikh. "Though innocent of any crime, thou hast condemned him to die. Is it not written in the Book of Everlasting Will that mercy should be shown unto the weak?"

"He is a Roumi, and his tribe will be consumed by the unquenchable fire in Al-Hawiyat," answered the chief of the rebels.

"Of a verity thou speakest the truth," she said. "But is it not also written that thou shalt not transgress by attacking the infidel first, for Allah loveth not the transgressors."

"I have spoken!" roared the Sheikh in anger. "Seek not to argue, but return unto thy divan. The son of a dog shall die!" and, pushing her roughly aside, he strode into his tent amid the murmured approbation of the crowd of dark-visaged horsemen who had assembled.

"Brothers," she cried in a voice that betrayed her agitation, "the Roumi now before thee hath fallen into our hands, therefore we should show him mercy. I, Halima Fathma, daughter of thy Sheikh,—upon whom may the One Merciful pour abundant blessing—appeal unto thee on his behalf. Wilt thou not release him, and lift from my heart the weight which oppresseth it?"

In the silence that followed, she gazed appealingly around.

"No," they answered, when they had whispered among themselves. "Our Sheikh hath condemned the spy. He seeketh to betray us, and must die."

"I am hungry," I cried, as, after further vain argument, the Sheikh's daughter was turning away. "It is permissible, I suppose, to have a last meal?"

Saying this, I stopped, and, picking up the small loaf which the Arabs had taken from my saddle-bag, commenced to eat it with a coolness which apparently astonished the group of freebooters of the plains.

Through that balmy moonlit night I remained where my captors had left me, bound to a palm tree in the vicinity of the settlement. Hour after hour I waited alone, watching the beauty of the Oriental sky, and longing for the end. I knew I should receive no quarter—that ere the sun rose I should be shot down, and my body left to the vultures. My thoughts reverted to my boyhood, to my gay, reckless career in Paris, and most of all to Valerie.

The moon was fast disappearing, and I was calmly watching for the steely-grey light which in the desert is precursory of dawn, when suddenly I heard a footstep. The person was concealed behind some huge boulders, and I concluded that it was one of my captors who had mounted guard over me.

Yet, as I listened, the steps sounded too stealthy, like those of a light-footed thief. I stood breathless in wonderment, when suddenly a slim, white-robed figure crept from behind the rocks, and advanced towards me.

It was an Arab youth. He placed his finger upon his lips, indicative of silence.

As he came up to me, I gazed at him in surprise, for his haick concealed his face.

"Hush!" he whispered in Arabic; "make no noise, or we may be discovered. It is cruel that a brave officer like thyself should be murdered," he added. "I have come to save thee."

"How didst thou know I was an officer?"

"Ask no questions," he replied. And drawing a keen knife from beneath his burnouse, he severed the cords that bound me.

"Thou art free," he said. "Come, follow me."

Picking up the bread I had not eaten, I thrust it into my pocket, and followed my unknown friend up a stony path that led into a narrow mountain pass. When some distance from the settlement, we came to a clump of trees, to one of which was tethered my camel.

"Quick! Mount and ride away," he urged. "Keep straight through the pass, and when thou gainest the desert, turn at once towards the north. A day's journey from here will bring thee unto the encampment of thy comrades."

"Only a day's journey!" I cried. "To what do I owe the sudden interest that the daughter of the Sheikh hath taken in my welfare?" I asked, laughing.

"I know not. Women have such strange caprices sometimes. But get away quickly," he urged. "Lose not a moment, or thou wilt be overtaken. *Slama. Alah iselemeck!*"

Turning from me, he hurried away; not, however, before I had discerned in the faint grey light that the face, half hidden by the spotless haick surrounding it, was beardless, evidently that of a woman. Was it Halima herself?

At first I was prompted to follow and ascertain; but next second I saw the grave risks we both were running, and, mounting my swift *meheri*, started off at a gallop over the rough stones and dunes of loose, treacherous sand.

Suddenly the crack of a rifle startled me. Then, as I glanced back, I saw, to my amazement and dismay, the slim, burnoused figure lying in a heap upon the stones; while three yelling, gesticulating Arabs were standing over it, cursing, brandishing their knives and shaking their fists. Evidently they had shot my rescuer!

To linger, however, would mean death. Therefore, on emerging from the pass, I took the route described by the mysterious person who had given me my freedom; galloping over the trackless desert in a northerly direction, with eyes eager to discern the encampment of Spahis and Zouaves.

Before nightfall I was safe within the French lines, relating to General Le Pelletier the events of my journey, and explaining the perilous position of the 39th Regiment.

"But you mentioned something of dispatches, and a plan of the country?" he said.

"Yes; I have them here," I replied.

Then, taking from my pocket the half-eaten roll of bread, I broke it, and took therefrom two small pieces of paper.

One was a map in miniature, showing the route he was to travel, and the other the dispatch.

"WE ARE CLOSE UPON THEM now," I remarked to an officer riding by my side on the next night. "They'll fight like demons."

Hardly had the words passed my lips, before wild yells of rage rent the air on every side; and ere we could realise it, we had surprised the encampment of the Kel-Ahamellen, and rifles flashed on every side.

I need not describe the desperate hand-to-hand conflict in the darkness. Suffice it to say, that we punished the tribe for their temerity in sentencing me to death.

When in the early morning, after a severe engagement, we walked among the ruins of the tents and heaps of dead, I searched diligently for Halima, being aided by a dozen other officers and men. But we did not discover her; and I became convinced that my worst fears were realised, and that she had fallen a victim to the relentless vengeance of her people.

NEARLY TWO YEARS ELAPSED BEFORE I again trod the asphalte of my beloved Paris.

A few weeks after my return to civilisation, I attended a ball at the

German Embassy. I had been dancing, and was taking my partner, a rather skittish widow, into the supper-room, when I accidentally stepped upon and rent the dress-train of a dark-haired girl, who, leaning upon the arm of an elderly man, was walking before me.

She turned, and I bowed my apologies. The words died from my lips.

The woman, whose flower-trimmed dress I had torn, was Valerie! It was a mutual recognition; but neither of us spoke.

Half an hour later, however, I was sitting alone with her. To my fierce demands for an explanation of the sudden breaking off of her communications, she replied boldly, and with such an air of veracity that I hated myself for having spoken so harshly.

Judge my joy when she told me she was still unmarried, that the paragraph in the *Figaro* was unauthorised, and that it had been inserted by some unknown enemy, during her absence from Paris.

"Then you are not Madame Delbet?" I cried, with ill-concealed delight.

"Certainly not; M'sieur Delbet is an old friend of our family, that is all," she replied, laughing. "After you left Oran, I could not write, as you were away in the desert. I read of your adventures and your bravery in the newspapers, but did not know where a letter would find you; therefore, I left all explanations of my enforced silence until your return."

"And—you still love me?" I asked, with trepidation, placing my arm tenderly around her slim waist, and drawing her towards me.

"Of course. But, *mon cher*, you have never doubted me, have you?"

"No," I replied, after an awkward pause, gazing fondly into her eyes. "But now I have gained my promotion, will you become my wife?"

Her answer was affirmative, and we sealed our compact with a kiss.

WOULD THAT I COULD OMIT this last and terrible chapter of my biography. But no! The hideous story must be related to its bitter end, to serve as warning to others.

Through closed windows and drawn curtains was borne the solemn clang of a bell in a church tower in the Avenue de Villiers, recording the death of to-day and the birth of to-morrow. A simple canary in its gilded cage, mistaking for morning sunshine the soft glow of electricity, as it filtered through its shade of orange silk, chirped a matin song in shrill staccato. A tiny slippered foot nervously patted the sleek fur of the tiger rug beneath it, a strong arm girt a slender waist; and, between the solemn strokes of the church bell, and the cheery passages of the bird-song, quick, passionate kisses alone stirred the scented air.

The man spoke. It was Rene Delbet!

"I must go now, darling," he said. "We have both braved too much already. He may return at any moment."

"And if he did?" Valerie asked defiantly.

"He might at least—suspect."

"Suspect?" and she laughed a chorus to the canary. "He doesn't know what suspicion means. He would trust me with Mephistopheles himself. Should he find you here, he would only thank you for entertaining me. He's the most easy-going fellow in the world."

The man smiled, released his companion from his embrace, and rose from the settee, upon which the two had been seated.

"I'm afraid, my dear," he said, "that you presume too much upon his confidence. There is no cord so elastic that it will not snap."

I waited for no more, but burst into the room, having, in my frenzy of madness, drawn a revolver from my pocket.

"*Diable*! You?" cried Delbet, starting up in alarm.

"Ah, my husband!" gasped Valerie, covering her blanched face with her hands.

"*Sacre*! You shall die!" I shouted.

The tolling bell throbbed once again, and then—a short, sharp, loud report and a flash together. A little puff of blue-grey smoke floated ceilingward, a man's frightened cry pierced the night, and upon the harmonious colours of the flower-strewn carpet Valerie lay dead.

RUSHING TO MY WIFE'S BOUDOIR, I broke open her escritoire, bent upon ascertaining the nature of any letters she might have concealed there.

There were many. Ah, *Dieu*! When I think of the passionate love-missives penned by the man whom I had implicitly trusted, and admitted to my home as a friend, my brain is lashed to frenzy.

One discovery I made was startling. Several of the letters bore the stamp of twenty-five centimes, and their envelopes were addressed to "Mademoiselle Halima Fathma, care of Hadj Hassan, Douera Algerie."

Searching further, I discovered a full-length cabinet photograph, taken in Algiers. It was of Valerie dressed as the Sheikh's daughter, with the exception that the *adjar*, which had hidden the Arab girl's face, had been removed.

In my surprise I almost forgot the terrible tragedy.

Continuing the investigation of the odds and ends in her private drawer, I found an Arab head ornament and several bracelets. The pattern of the crescent-shaped sequins I recognised as the same as those worn by the mysterious Halima.

These discoveries, combined with the contents of the letters which I hastily scanned, left no doubt that Halima and Valerie were the same person; and, further, that Hassan, the wealthy Sheikh of the Ahamellen, who had a house at Douera, was really her father; and that Monsieur de Noirville had brought her up, and educated her to the ways of civilised society.

When I had left for Algeria, it had been her caprice to follow me, and rejoin her people.

She had saved my life, yet I had killed her.

But though so fair, she was false—*false*!

BAH! HOW INFERNALLY BITTER THIS cognac is!

One more gulp, and my body and soul will have parted. I shall be at rest.

Ah, well! Here's health to the cursed scoundrel who has wrecked my life. The glass is drained. The sediment was like gall.

How it burns!

I—I go. I trouble no one longer. *Au revoir. Adieu!*

A Note About the Author

William Le Queux (1864–1927) was an Anglo-French journalist, novelist, and radio broadcaster. Born in London to a French father and English mother, Le Queux studied art in Paris and embarked on a walking tour of Europe before finding work as a reporter for various French newspapers. Towards the end of the 1880s, he returned to London where he edited *Gossip* and *Piccadilly* before being hired as a reporter for *The Globe* in 1891. After several unhappy years, he left journalism to pursue his creative interests. Le Queux made a name for himself as a leading writer of popular fiction with such espionage thrillers as *The Great War in England in 1897* (1894) and *The Invasion of 1910* (1906). In addition to his writing, Le Queux was a notable pioneer of early aviation and radio communication, interests he maintained while publishing around 150 novels over his decades long career.

A Note from the Publisher

Spanning many genres, from non-fiction essays to literature classics to children's books and lyric poetry, Mint Edition books showcase the master works of our time in a modern new package. The text is freshly typeset, is clean and easy to read, and features a new note about the author in each volume. Many books also include exclusive new introductory material. Every book boasts a striking new cover, which makes it as appropriate for collecting as it is for gift giving. Mint Edition books are only printed when a reader orders them, so natural resources are not wasted. We're proud that our books are never manufactured in excess and exist only in the exact quantity they need to be read and enjoyed.

Discover more of your favorite classics with Bookfinity™.

- Track your reading with custom book lists.
- Get great book recommendations for your personalized Reader Type.
- Add reviews for your favorite books.
- AND MUCH MORE!

Visit **bookfinity.com** and take the fun Reader Type quiz to get started.

Enjoy our classic and modern companion pairings!